INDIGO'S DRAGON

SOFI CROFT

Published by Accent Press Ltd 2016

ISBN 9781783759385

For Nicky and Alec, and all who love dragons and stories.

Thank you!

CHAPTER ONE

AN UNEXPECTED PARCEL

Indigo stood on the top of Great Crag and gazed at the mountains that rolled away in every direction as far as he could see. He lifted his arms up and out and felt the breeze flowing between his fingers. If someone told him at that moment he could stay on the fells forever, he would have jumped at the chance.

He sat down, took his shoes and socks off, and studied the valley below him. Long and narrow, it ran west to east. The beck shone silver as it cut through the fields. His house was a tiny white dot, set apart from more tiny white dots that made up the village.

Indigo looked up from the valley to the slate-topped mountains in the east. He searched for signs of a cave. When he was young his mother had told him a slate dragon lived there. She said she'd played with the dragon as a young girl in Poland, and that the dragon had followed her here, but now it was in a deep sleep. Indigo didn't believe in dragons anymore, but he did believe there were marvellous places to be explored in the mountains that rose and fell around him.

He lifted his head to the clear blue sky. The rock was warm beneath his bare feet and he pushed his toes down onto the rough surface. A glint of sunshine reflected on something in the valley below, catching his eye. A small red van was heading along the rough single track road towards the village. Indigo remembered his mother's instructions the night before, *'Don't go out until the postman's been, I'm expecting a parcel.'* He wouldn't reach his house before the postman, but he might catch him before he left the village. Indigo took a deep breath, turned, and started to run.

The path dropped steeply into a shaded oak forest. Indigo's bare feet skimmed over cool slate slabs arranged in uneven steps. Halfway down the mountain Indigo jumped, grabbed a thick branch growing overhead, and swung onto a mossy mound further down the trail. He straightened and paused to catch his breath. His toes sank into cool, wet moss and he looked down. A shaft of sunlight broke through the canopy, illuminating the moss a bright, brilliant green. Indigo flexed his toes and carried on running.

He ran faster as the trail became less steep and rocky and more mossy and grassy. The world whizzed past him in a blur of greens, browns, and greys. His feet barely touched the floor; he felt almost weightless. He swung out his arms like wings and soared … then his bare feet squelched into wet, slimy grass as he pelted down the last hill towards the village.

When Indigo reached the gravel path on the valley floor he regretted leaving his shoes behind. Every step was painful as he picked his way across the small, sharp rocks. He turned the corner onto the road and felt relieved, because it would be easier on his feet, and because he could see the post van parked outside Ivy Cottage. He jogged to the van, and reached it at the same time as the postman did.

'I signed for your mum's parcel and left it in your kitchen.' The postman leaned towards Indigo and lowered his voice, 'I wouldn't leave your door open anymore if I were you. There was a break-in at the library last night.'

'A break in?' Indigo was shocked. He had never heard of a break in, or any other kind of crime, in the area. Besides, the library was the oddest place to break into; there weren't even many books in it. 'What did they take?'

'Nothing. They broke the locks, though.' The postman shook his head in dismay, 'Mrs Wood says it feels all cold and strange in there now, not safe. She's taken some time off.' He climbed into his van, 'Well, the weather's warming, make the most of it.'

'I will.' Indigo's voice was drowned out by the engine, and the postman drove off with a smile and a nod.

Indigo walked around to the back of his house. A loud *smack* made him jump as something hit the back door. A plume of soft white feathers floated in the air and droplets of fresh blood spattered the slate slab.

Two large birds were fighting in the air. The biggest magpie Indigo had ever seen opened its black beak and cackled as it aimed its claws at the bird beneath it. Something was strange about the back of the magpie, but before Indigo could take a good look he was distracted by the other bird. Its wings were made of stretched skin and Indigo realised it wasn't a bird, but a huge bat. It had big black ears, yellow eyes, and a screwed-up nose above a small mouth filled with sharp, white teeth. Its mouth opened in a silent scream as it twisted in the air to avoid the magpie's claws. The bat glanced at Indigo as it flew off, and Indigo wondered what it was thinking. It had seemed to give him a meaningful look, although he had no idea what the bat meant by it – or if it even meant anything at all.

The magpie landed on the barn roof behind his house. Indigo stared at it and it stared back with shiny black eyes. It was entirely black with a white belly – like a normal magpie. Then it became strange. Instead of black tail feathers it had a back end with short white fur and a long, curved, white tail, gently whipping like a cat's. Indigo thought he could make out two furry back paws, but he decided it must be a trick of the light. He raised his hand to shield his eyes from the glare, and as he did so, the bird opened its wings and flew off behind the barn, taking its strange back end with it.

Indigo opened the door and saw two parcels on the kitchen table. One was a red cardboard box stating it was *URGENT* and *FRAGILE*. His mother received lots of parcels like this. The other was wrapped in waxy brown paper, and tied with frayed brown string. It looked like it had been sent from the past.

Indigo drew closer and tilted his head to read the inky black writing. His name and address were written in English, but the ornate penmanship gave the impression of an ancient, foreign language.

Indigo Wawelski
Stonecroft Cottage
Underthwaite
Lake District
UK

Indigo was excited. He hardly ever received parcels. Sometimes he got one on his birthday, but that was months away. He put his fingers on the paper and it crackled. It was definitely addressed to him. He untied the string.

Inside was a faded brown leather satchel with brass buckles. Indigo recognised it at once. It belonged to his grandfather, Opi. He fingered the soft leather and a lump rose in his throat. *Did this mean something had happened to Opi?*

As far back as Indigo could remember Opi had visited once a year, in autumn. He would sit by the fire and tell stories about amazing and impossible beasts that lived in the Polish mountains near his home. His stories usually involved a rescue; a dragon with a wound that needed dressing, a sasquatch with sore feet, an unconscious giant who had fallen from a great height, or a unicorn with hornache. Opi would pull things from his satchel to illustrate his stories; a dragon's tooth, a dried-up tentacle, or a griffin feather. *A griffin feather!* The bird outside had resembled a griffin, but instead of half-eagle and half-lion it had seemed to be half-magpie and half-cat. Indigo wondered what Opi would call a creature like that. He decided it didn't matter. It had been years since Indigo had believed Opi's stories. He was thirteen now. Too old for stories.

Indigo unbuckled the satchel, but hesitated. It felt wrong opening Opi's bag. It contained his personal possessions, his most treasured things. He fastened the buckles, and took the bag to his bedroom. He wondered who had sent it to him, and why. Maybe it would contain a letter, a note of explanation. He thought that perhaps he should look inside after all.

4

CHAPTER TWO

THE NOT-A-GRIFFIN

Indigo sat on his bed and stared at the satchel. *Boom!* A gunshot jolted him from his thoughts. The farmer was shooting magpies again. Panic surged in Indigo's chest as he remembered the magpie-cat.

He flew down the stairs and burst through the back door in time to see the farmer standing near the barn, gun raised, aiming at something on the far side of the field. *Boom!* Another shot echoed down the valley, muting as it bounced off each of the fells.

The farmer turned to Indigo, 'Got it!'

'What was it?'

'Magpie. Didn't you see it over on that post? It was massive. Biggest one I've ever seen. I reckon it killed two lambs this week. Nasty piece of work.' The farmer rested his gun on his shoulder.

Indigo wanted to ask if it had a strange back end, but he just said, 'Oh.'

'You got a catapult?'

Indigo shook his head, 'No.'

'When I was your age, I used to take them out with a catapult. I'll see if I can find you one. You could make yourself useful while you're in the valley all day.' The farmer raised his eyebrows, 'Are you ever going back to school?'

Indigo shook his head again, 'I didn't like being cooped up in a classroom.'

The farmer smiled. 'I can relate to that.'

Indigo scanned the field, searching for the dead bird.

'Well, back to it.' The farmer locked his gun in his tractor and plodded off to the lambing shed.

Indigo wandered across the field. The ewes backed away from him and the lambs watched him curiously. A loud cackle shook the air. Indigo stopped, and turned to the noise. It softened to a feeble growl. He headed for the fence posts, and the cackling became more frequent. It didn't take him long to spot the creature.

It was, in part, a magpie, but its whole was not a magpie. It was more than a magpie. The word that came into Indigo's head was 'griffin', although it was not a griffin either.

The not-a-griffin lay crumpled in a wet, muddy ditch, leaning to one side and holding its wing out awkwardly. It appeared shocked and confused. Indigo's first thoughts were how he could help it. He knew it needed to be kept calm, and checked over for injuries.

Indigo stepped over the fence and moved towards the creature slowly, making soft shushing noises. The creature watched him with shiny black eyes. Indigo crouched low and examined it. The magpie's head was fine, but there was obviously something wrong with the wing it was holding out; where the wing connected to the body there was a damp mangled area.

'Did it get your wing?' Indigo whispered.

The creature opened its beak, as if it were going to say something, then tilted its head, and remained silent. Its wing trembled, and streaks of blue and purple iridescence shone in the sunlight. Underneath the wing, white feathers gave way to short white fur. It had the back end of a cat, complete with two legs, clawed paws, and a long white tail that writhed in and out of the mud. The creature *was* half-magpie and half-cat.

'Shush now, you'll be all right, it's all right, kitty.' Indigo eyed the creature's belly, deciding where to place his hands. Then, with a swift and sure movement, he reached out, picked it up, and folded it into his arms against his chest. Its wings flapped clumsily. Indigo felt its beak stab into his hand and claws scratch his body, but he didn't flinch. 'Shush, kitty. There's no need for that.' He held the creature firm and close and it settled. It was cold, wet, and surprisingly heavy. Indigo rose to his feet and carried it home.

Indigo laid the magpie-cat on his bed. It remained still – even its tail had stopped swishing. He picked a fleece jumper from the floor and covered it. Opi's satchel caught his eye. *It would contain a first aid kit.* Indigo opened the bag and rummaged inside. There was a notebook, a bundle of feathers, binoculars, a small round tin, and a wooden box painted green. Indigo took out the box and opened it. Sixteen little brown glass bottles were in individual compartments. Each bottle had a lid of a different colour and shape. Indigo pulled a couple out and saw the labels were handwritten in Polish. He slid them back into their compartments, put the box on the bed, and carried on rummaging. He found a soft leather pouch, a hip flask, and a battered red tin with a white cross on it.

Indigo was about to open the red tin when the magpie-cat lifted its head and reached towards the wooden box. Indigo pushed the box closer. The magpie-cat pulled a bottle with a triangular white lid out of the box, dropped it on the bed, and stared at Indigo.

Indigo picked up the bottle and read the label: *Yarrow Antyseptyczny.* Indigo didn't know much Polish, but he realised *Antyseptyczny* probably meant antiseptic. He opened the lid. A tiny spray cap was underneath.

'Clever bird, clever kitty.' He pulled the fleece back and peered at the wound. 'The bullet just grazed you.' Indigo aimed the bottle and squirted twice. Tiny droplets covered the wound and a pleasant herb smell filled the air. 'You'll be flying away in no time.'

As the magpie-cat lay down its head, Indigo pulled the fleece back up and a deep purring noise emanated from its belly.

Indigo delved deeper into the satchel. There were old leather gloves, new rubber gloves, a roll of plastic film, a bottle of glue, a bag of dried yellow flowers, some unfamiliar metal tools wrapped in a yellow duster, and a torch. No note.

Indigo opened the red tin. It contained first aid equipment; bandages, dressings, scissors, tweezers, and a needle and thread.

The small round tin contained teeth; a mixture of what looked like translucent human milk teeth and curved, sharp, pointed teeth from some unknown carnivore.

Indigo put everything back inside the satchel, except the notebook. He fastened the buckles, slid the bag under his bed, and picked up the book. It was small but thick, with a soft green leather cover and shining gold page edges. Curved and crooked gold writing luminesced on the front.

Okkup Bezzesss

Indigo didn't recognise the words. They didn't even seem Polish. He opened the book and everything slowed; his breathing, his heart, the purring of the magpie-cat, even the dust specks in the air floated more calmly. Everything was still and quiet.

Then the bubbles formed. Bubbles of excitement that grew in Indigo's belly. They rose to his head, bursting into sparks, and sank to his fingers and toes, making them tingle and twitch as he gazed at the yellowed pages covered in curved and crooked black ink.

Indigo didn't understand the words, but there were tiny ink drawings all around the page edges, washed with hints of colour. There was a blood red egg with yellow spots; a yellow and black snake with big red eyes, a huge red beak, and a cockerel's comb on its head; a snake with scaly legs and feathered wings; a plant with clusters of small yellow flowers; gloves, and a blindfold.

Indigo flicked through the book, glancing over the myriads of ink drawings. Mythical monsters and unbelievable beasts were all carefully drawn alongside pictures of plants, flowers, bottles, dressings, metal tools, and safety equipment.

'Indigo! I'm home!' His mother's voice cut through the air and he dropped the book. As the pages fanned shut he thought he saw a picture on the page edges – a lady in a castle, a dragon in a cave, and a man carrying a sheep – but then his mother shouted his name again. He slid the book under his pillow and went downstairs.

Indigo's mother, Emerald, was in the kitchen making a mug of tea. Her hair was a mass of red curls and she smelled of cocoa butter.

'Have you had lunch?'

'Yes,' Indigo lied.

Emerald picked up her parcel. 'Was there any other post?'

'No,' Indigo lied again. He didn't know why.

'So what have you been up to?' Emerald smiled.

'I walked up to Great Crag.' Indigo felt better telling a truth.

'Oh, good. Nice day for it.'

'What about you?' Indigo realised he didn't know where his mother had been.

'What about me?' She sipped her tea.

'What have you been doing?'

'Oh you know, boring stuff. Your dad and Safi will be back soon, I'll make dinner,' Emerald wandered off with her tea and her parcel.

Indigo returned to his bedroom. The magpie-cat was not on his bed. He scanned his room. He looked out of the window. Sparrows flew from the bird feeder to the hedge. There was no sign of the magpie-cat.

Indigo suddenly felt very alarmed. He bent down and looked under his bed. The satchel was gone too. A wave of nausea hit him. He grabbed a torch from his bedside table and pointed it under the bed. The beam of light illuminated clumps of dust. The satchel wasn't there.

Indigo looked under clothes abandoned on the floor, behind his shelves, in his wardrobe, behind his door – all the while the dull ache in his stomach telling him they were gone. He looked in the other rooms upstairs; his parents' bedroom, Safi's bedroom, the bathroom. There was no sign of the satchel, and no sign of the magpie-cat.

Indigo raced down the stairs, frantically trying to work out where the magpie-cat and the satchel might be.

'I left my shoes on Great Crag,' he blurted out as he passed his mother chopping vegetables in the kitchen, and charged through the back door.

Indigo searched outside the house and around the barn. He walked across the field to where he had picked up the magpie-cat. There was no sign of the creature, or the bag. He decided to

9

head up the mountain; he could always see better from above. Maybe he would spot the magpie-cat, maybe it had taken the bag – maybe he would find them both.

Indigo neither saw nor heard the magpie-cat as he climbed the mountain. His worn-out trainers were abandoned on the peak, and he sat next to them to survey the valley. Everything was grey in the approaching dusk. The sense of elation he'd felt earlier was gone. He was confused, uneasy, and ashamed he hadn't told his mother about the satchel. He needed to find out if Opi was all right.

He thought about the magpie-cat and the huge bat. It was as though they'd flown straight out of one of Opi's stories about strange beasts in the Polish mountains. Indigo wondered if the Tatras were anything like the Lake District. Opi had told him the Tatras were much higher, but he knew there were similarities – dramatic views, forests, lakes, rivers, and waterfalls. Both were landscapes you could get lost in.

Indigo was walking down the last grassy hill before the village when the bat flew past him so close he felt his hair part. It was carrying something round and red. The bat swooped low to the ground in front of Indigo, and dropped the object. It rolled a few metres before coming to rest in a boggy spot. The bat flew off, and Indigo walked towards the object.

It was an egg. About the size of an apple, blood red with yellow spots. Just like the drawing in Opi's book. Indigo picked it up. It was smooth and hard. Not knowing what else to do, he carried it home.

CHAPTER THREE

LOST IN A LIBRARY

Indigo put the egg on his bed and checked under his pillow. The book was still there. He slid it out, opened it, and searched the first page for words he might understand. There were none. He studied the pictures. There was the egg – red with yellow spots, identical to the egg on his bed. Underneath were drawings of creatures that could presumably hatch out of the egg. They were part snake and part cockerel. Indigo had read about mythical beasts like this. They were called cockatrices and basilisks, and were poisonous. In fact, Indigo remembered, they could kill with a single look.

At the bottom of the page was a drawing of a plant with small yellow flowers. *Rue* was written next to it, with drawings of a bucket, gloves, and blindfold beneath it.

'Indigo! Dinner!' For the second time that day his mother's voice made him drop the book, and for the second time that day Indigo thought he saw a picture on the page edges as it fell. He picked up the book. The edge was gold, but faded and dull. No picture. He replaced it under his pillow and went downstairs.

'Are Dad and Safi back?' Indigo asked.

'The car just pulled in. Will you serve?' Emerald took her tea to the table.

Indigo put the first plateful of food in front of his mother. The back door opened and Safi walked in, her hair wet and her skin translucent.

'That smells good.' She leaned close to the wall and held the door open so their father, Marek, could wheel himself in.

'It does smell good.' Marek glided into the room and landed a kiss on Emerald before swivelling his chair under the table. He had the same damp, translucent appearance as Safi. 'Serve it up, Indigo,' he smiled.

Indigo put a plate in front of him, 'Good diving?'

'Beautiful. Spring has arrived under the waves,' Marek looked at Indigo, but anyone could tell he was fifty miles away, under the sea.

Safi took a plate and sat down. 'You should come with us tomorrow. We have a fantastic itinerary planned. Five dives: a drift dive, a cave dive, a shipwreck, diving with seals, and a night dive.'

'That does sound amazing, but I've got a few things to do.' Indigo was thinking about the egg upstairs. If it was a cockatrice egg, and if the myths were true, then when it hatched the cockatrice would kill everything it looked at. He needed to get a box – a strong metal box with a lock, gloves, a blindfold, and a bucketful of Rue – whatever that was.

The dinner was interrupted by a resounding *boom*! Everything wobbled slightly and Indigo wondered if a plane had crashed nearby. Emerald dashed to the coat hooks and threw on her waterproofs.

'Was that an earthquake?' Safi asked, her mouth full of food.

'Don't talk with your mouth full. It might have been. I have to pop out.' Emerald tightened the laces of her hiking boots, 'There's chocolate ice cream in the freezer.'

Marek turned to Emerald, 'Are you going to check on Mrs Wood?'

Emerald looked at him in confusion for a moment, then her face relaxed, 'Yes, she'll need company. I might be late back,' Emerald walked round the table, kissed everyone in turn, and disappeared out of the back door.

'Was it an earthquake?' Safi asked again, this time her mouth empty.

'I imagine so.' Marek scooped some food into his mouth. He was fifty miles away again, watching flotsam bobbing on the waves.

When Indigo went to bed that night his mother hadn't returned, but he wasn't thinking about where she was. His mind was focused entirely on the egg, now nestled on a fleece jumper under his bed.

In the middle of the night, Indigo was still awake. He crept downstairs, went outside, and took a strong metal box from the tool shed. Back in his bedroom he exchanged the tools in the box for the cockatrice egg. He locked the box, pushed it under his bed, and slept soundly.

No-one was home when Indigo woke the next morning. He made toast and decided to go to the library to find out what Rue was.

The library was on the outskirts of the next village, a couple of miles away. The sky was blue, the sun was shining, and the lambs in the fields glowed a dazzling white. Most of them wobbled near their mothers, but a few had ventured further and were skipping and bleating in the exhilaration of independence.

Indigo daydreamed as he walked; he thought about all the stories Opi had told him, all the creatures he had described. The cockatrice egg was real, and that meant it was possible all the creatures from Opi's stories were real too.

Excitement surged inside Indigo, and by the time he saw the library, a concrete box out of place in a valley of old stone cottages, he was running.

Indigo slowed to a walk, and remembered the break in. He was relieved to find the sign on the library door read "Open".

The librarian, Mrs Wood, was not at her desk. Indigo walked up to the young girl sitting in her place. She had pale skin, dark hair, and wore black, old-fashioned clothing at odds with the colourful, modern library.

'Hi,' Indigo said.

'Can I help you?' The girl didn't glance up from her book.

'I'm looking for a book on healing herbs, and how to use them.'

'You'll only find basic gardening books up here. Why don't you ask Dr Orava in the archives? All the most interesting books are down there.' The corners of her mouth twitched as she nodded to a door behind Indigo. A sign on it read "Keep Out".

The door was heavier than Indigo expected. Narrow stone steps led steeply down into gloom below, and the air became cooler and damper as Indigo descended. At the bottom of the steps was an archway. Indigo walked through into a massive stone room, at least three times the size of the library above. Warm, dry air enveloped him, along with the intense smell of old books. The room was full of tall, dark wooden shelves crammed with books and papers.

'Wow.' Indigo realised he had spoken out loud and coughed.

'It's impressive, isn't it?' A tall, thin man with a long, pale face and smooth black hair walked towards Indigo. He wore a shiny black suit and a cravat. 'I am Dr Skuba Gyorgy Orava.' He held out his hand. Long, yellowing nails protruded from his long, white fingers.

Indigo stared at him, speechless.

'And you are?' Dr Orava's claw-like hand was still extended towards Indigo. He smiled with closed lips. The smile didn't reach his yellow eyes.

Indigo took Orava's cold hand. Orava's grip tightened, and he held on for longer than was comfortable, staring at Indigo. Icy rivulets snaked up Indigo's arm and he pulled away.

'Indigo Wawelski,' he replied.

'Wawelski,' Orava's yellow eyes narrowed, 'you are related to Smok?'

'Smok?' Indigo hadn't heard that name.

'How can I help you, Indigo?' Orava examined the back of his hand, as if it might have picked up dirt.

'The girl upstairs said you might help me find a book on healing herbs, and how to use them.' Indigo's instinct was to run, but he was frozen to the stone floor.

'Yes, I can help you.' Orava stared, unblinking at Indigo.

Indigo looked away.

Orava turned on his heel and walked to the shelves behind him. He crouched low and his long fingers danced over the books on the bottom shelf. 'What about this?' He held out a fat leather-bound volume.

Indigo leaned forward and read the title, *Medicinal and Magical Herbalism*. He reached out to take the book, but Orava withdrew it out of his reach. 'You can read it here. Books from the archives are not for loan.' He strode to a large wooden desk in a corner, placed the book on it, and walked away.

Indigo sat on a stool in front of the desk and opened the book. He was reading the contents, searching for "Rue", when Orava's icy fingers grabbed his shoulder, making him jump.

'Is there a particular remedy you're looking for, Indigo?'

'Rue.' The word fell out of Indigo's mouth involuntarily.

Orava leaned over Indigo's shoulder, his long nails digging into Indigo's skin through his clothes, and thumbed through the pages of the book. He opened it on a page with a watercolour painting of a leafy green plant with small yellow flowers. 'Rue has been cultivated for its medicinal uses in English gardens since Roman times, Indigo. I would be surprised if your mother didn't have some in her garden.'

'You know my mother?' Again, the words fell out of Indigo's mouth before he realised what he was saying.

'Emerald. Yes, of course,' Orava let go of Indigo's shoulder and inspected his fingernails. 'We know something of each other.'

'I haven't seen you before, or the girl upstairs,' Indigo ventured.

Orava waved Indigo's comment away. 'There are few people in this valley, Indigo, and even fewer people like us.'

'Like us?'

Orava raised his eyebrows. 'People with Polish roots, Indigo.'

Indigo shifted uncomfortably on his stool. He came here to learn about rue, not talk about roots.

'I am from the same place as your grandparents, Indigo. Wanda and I were friends in Krakow,' Orava's eyes glazed over.

'You know my grandmother? Do you know my grandfather too?'

Orava put his hand over his heart, as if he had a sudden attack of heartburn. 'I think you need to ask your mother, Indigo.'

'Ask my mother?'

'About the rue.'

'Oh. The rue. You think she will have some?'

'Almost certainly. It's strange you didn't ask her in the first

15

place.'

Indigo suddenly felt guilty. He should have asked his mother instead of coming here; she would know about rue. Orava leaned over Indigo again, and shut the book. Indigo had an overwhelming urge to leave. He ducked under Orava's arm and backed towards the stairs, 'Thank you, Dr Orava.'

Orava held out a small card. 'My number, Indigo. In case you need anything.'

Indigo took the card and raced up the stairs two at a time. A metallic laugh followed him, but when Indigo stood in the cool fresh air outside the library, he wondered if it had simply been a ringing in his ears.

CHAPTER FOUR

THE COCKATRICE

Indigo walked home feeling uncomfortable. His skin was crawling, he had a bitter taste in his mouth, and a grey fog surrounded his head. He was over half way home before the fog lifted and he started to feel more like himself.

Light footsteps accelerated behind Indigo and he spun around. The girl from the library was behind him. She looked him in the eyes and the corners of her mouth twitched.

'You could just destroy it, you know.'

'I couldn't do that,' Indigo said, horrified she had suggested it and confused as to how she knew about the egg.

'Why not?' she challenged.

Indigo carried on walking. The egg contained a rare and extraordinary creature. He couldn't destroy it.

The girl followed him. 'You do realise how dangerous it is, don't you?'

Indigo stopped, 'Who are you?'

'Rue.'

'Rue?'

'That's my name, Rue, like the plant.'

Indigo noticed her light brown eyes were flecked with yellow, 'Is Orava your father?'

'No. Do you want my help or not?'

'Your help?'

Rue rolled her eyes, 'Finding rue. The plant. Come on.' Rue walked to Indigo's front garden without saying another word. She scanned the plants growing in the flower beds. 'There,' she pointed to a low shrubby plant with small green leaves, 'pick some young leaves, and some shoots that haven't flowered yet, put a few handfuls in a bucketful of warm water, cover it with a cloth, and let it stand outside.'

'How long for?'

'As long as you can,' Rue raised her head.

Emerald was trudging up the track; her waterproofs were out of place on the sunny day, and they were streaked with white-grey dust from broken slate. She was clearly hot and bothered, but she smiled as she came into the garden, 'Hi, Indigo. Who's your friend?'

'Pleased to meet you, Mrs Wawelski,' Rue forced a smile, 'I came to ask for some rue for my grandmother, she thinks it helps her cataracts.'

Recognition spread across Emerald's face, and her eyebrows furrowed. 'Who's your grandmother?' she asked suspiciously.

Rue bent down, picked a few leaves, and smiled again. This time it was full of devilment. 'Mrs Wood. It was so good of you to check on her last night.'

Emerald gave Rue a hard stare.

'Thank you, Mrs Wawelski. See you, Indigo.' Rue walked away.

Emerald watched her leave. 'I'm not sure I like her.'

Indigo opened his mouth to say something in Rue's defence, but then noticed how tired his mother looked. Her curly red hair hung limp and knotted, and her eyes had grey shadows beneath them. 'Do you want a cup of tea?' he offered.

Emerald smiled and put her hand over her heart. 'I would love a cup of tea, Indigo.'

Emerald took her dusty waterproofs off as Indigo made the tea. 'Thanks, love. I need to phone into Krakow, then I'll make some sandwiches.' She took her tea and left the kitchen.

Relief washed over Indigo. His grandparents lived high in the Tatras and had no telephone. When his mother wanted to get in touch with them, she phoned a friend in Krakow who went to visit. It would take a day or two to hear back, but someone was going to check on Opi.

Indigo went to his bedroom, knelt down, and looked at the box under his bed. He listened. It was quiet. He slid the box out, and put his ear to the metal. Silence. He pushed it back under his bed and went downstairs. His mother was gone. There was a sandwich, a catapult, a bag of steel bearings, and a note on the kitchen table.

Farmer gave me the catapult for you.
I might be back late again.
Love you x

Indigo made Rue Water, following Rue's instructions, and left the covered bucket outside the back door. Then he picked up the catapult, took a handful of wizened acorns out of a decorative pot on the windowsill, and went for a walk.

He wandered up the valley to one of his favourite spots, where a series of small waterfalls and plunge pools lay hidden beneath twisted, overhanging oak trees.

Indigo sat under the biggest and most upright of the trees. He aimed acorns at rocks on the far side of the beck, challenging himself to hit them. The catapult was easy to use, and Indigo was soon aiming at rocks further and further away. He had just hit a rock about ten metres away when the bat flew past, heading towards the slate mountains in the east. Indigo tracked its flight, suppressing an urge to run after it. He considered following it, but decided it would be more sensible to go home and check the egg. Reluctantly, he turned and began walking home.

It was night when it happened. Indigo was studying a map of caves and tunnels he had found in the back of Opi's book when a faint sound, a ceramic scraping, rose from under his bed. Indigo went downstairs and returned with the bucket of Rue Water, gloves, and a black scarf.

Scrape! This time the noise was louder, and followed by a *hiss* and a strangled *cluck*. Indigo pulled the box out from beneath his bed. Something moved inside, throwing it off balance. Indigo remained calm. If he could get through the next ten minutes, everything would be all right. It would be safe again.

19

He tied the scarf as a blindfold around his forehead and put on the gloves. He slid the key in the lock, memorised the position of the box and the bucket, and lowered his blindfold. He knelt for a long time next to it, listening to the noises inside, visualising where the cockatrice was. Then he unlocked it.

He slipped both hands inside the box, into the corner he thought the cockatrice would be. He felt nothing. He swept his hands through the box, and grabbed something that cracked in his hands. *Shell.* Panic and dread suffocated Indigo. *The cockatrice wasn't in the box. It had escaped.* He held his breath and listened. Listened hard. Nothing.

The curtains swished softly in the wind, and Indigo realised the window was open. He felt his way to the sash, and pushed it down. Something stopped it from shutting, and a loud, pain-filled shriek rent the air.

Indigo grabbed the cockatrice. It whipped around, trapped in the sash. He gripped it tightly with both hands but it was too strong. It was a thick rope of muscle, determined to escape. It slipped away from him, out of the window. 'No!' Indigo shouted, but it was too late. It was gone.

Indigo pulled off his blindfold, grabbed his rucksack, ran downstairs and picked up the telephone. It only rang once before Orava answered – there was no time to change his mind.

'Dr Orava?'

'Indigo, how good to hear from you, I thought you might need my help.'

The line went dead.

Outside, the moon shone bright. Indigo closed his eyes and listened for a long time. A gentle breeze rustled the leaves and an owl hooted in the distance. When Indigo was sure he couldn't hear the cockatrice, he opened his eyes and glanced up at his bedroom window. A branch of a sycamore tree ran close to it. Indigo shone his torch on the branch. There was a black line, a scorched trail, as though fire had crept along the branch and down the tree, all the way to the bottom. The black path continued across the grass and under the garden gate. Indigo flinched as he saw Dr Orava standing behind the gate, staring at him.

'You let it escape.' Orava pointed one of his yellow finger claws at Indigo.

Indigo instantly regretted phoning him. 'What shall I do?'

'Do you have a trained weasel?'

'A weasel?'

Orava sighed melodramatically and inspected his fingernails. 'You always look so bewildered, Indigo.'

'I know where a stoat burrow is.'

'You are useless, Indigo, and I had such high hopes.'

Anger burned Indigo's cheeks and hands. 'I don't know why I phoned you.'

'I know,' Orava sounded disappointed. 'You can't do this without help.'

'I only wanted some advice.'

'To do what?' Orava scoffed. 'To follow a trail? It's burned into the ground!'

'I need a plan,' Indigo said firmly. 'At any moment the cockatrice could come out from behind a tree, and that would be it.'

'Oh, you are a smart boy, Indigo, so much smarter than you look.' Orava's teeth flashed in the moonlight and Indigo took a step back.

Orava smiled, 'Are you scared of me, Indigo?'

'No. You don't scare me, and I don't need your help.'

Orava's hand suddenly lurched over the gate, his claws flying towards Indigo's neck. Indigo jumped back and closed his eyes. Nothing touched him. He felt foolish. He opened his eyes, and saw Orava was gone.

Indigo followed the trail of scorched grass away from the village. On the grassy slope that led into the oak forest on the fellside the trail led behind a tree and disappeared.

Indigo crept closer. He closed his eyes and listened. Wind swished the long grass and stirred the leaves. A flutter of wings caused a brief commotion as a small bird flew out of the tree above him.

Silence fell. All Indigo could hear was his own breathing.

21

He took a small step forwards and something moved behind the tree, sliding quickly over grass. Dry skin grated against bark. Scales rasped over scales. The creature was coiling up in the roots of the tree.

Indigo took off his rucksack, crouched, and leaned towards the tree. He moved his hand slowly around the trunk, keeping his eyes tightly shut. *It doesn't want to hurt me.* Indigo clung to that thought as his hand darted downwards and he grabbed the cockatrice by the neck.

Back in his bedroom, Indigo pushed the whole rucksack into the bucket of Rue Water. The cockatrice didn't struggle. Indigo held it down for at least five minutes, and was wondering how long he should keep the cockatrice underwater when it began convulsing inside the bag.

Indigo lifted the bag out of the bucket and placed it on the floor. A puddle widened on the carpet. He unfastened the rucksack, leaned against the wall and closed his eyes. *If this doesn't work.* Indigo pushed the thought away by concentrating on the noises of the cockatrice. There was a wet spluttering cluck. Then a more confident *cluck*! Then a gentle hiss. It was moving towards him. Indigo steeled himself, breathed out slowly, and opened his eyes.

The cockatrice was the most beautifully ugly thing Indigo had ever seen. Its snake's body shone golden, and thin black lines marked intricate patterns along its back. Its head was raised high, travelling in an unfaltering straight line towards Indigo as its body moved sinuously behind. A spiked, fleshy comb stood proud on its head, passing between its huge red eyes and folding onto a wide, red beak that frowned disapprovingly at the corners.

Indigo laughed with relief. He was looking at a cockatrice and he was not dead. The pointed, downturned tip of its beak was inches away from his nose, and its eyes were level with his. They were enormous, perfectly round, with no pupils. All the shades of red in the world swirled in each eye. Indigo was transfixed. Somehow he understood how the cockatrice felt, destined to destroy everything it looked at, scorching the very ground it crossed. But now it was cured, able to look at another creature without killing it. They stared at each other for what could have been seconds or minutes. Then the cockatrice sank into Indigo's lap in a neat coil. Indigo put his hand on its back. It was cold and dry. He closed his eyes, and drifted into sleep.

CHAPTER FIVE

THE SLATE DRAGON

The sun was high in the sky when Indigo woke. He was stiff from sleeping on the floor. The cockatrice was curled untidily on his bed in a sunny patch, and Indigo could hear his dad and Safi talking in the front garden. He stood up, stretched, lifted the sash window, and leaned out.

Marek was rinsing his dry suit with a hose. It had been specially made with a long tail instead of legs. He said it was a gimmick, good for business.

'Sleeping beauty!' Marek shouted up at the window.

'Hi, Dad. Good diving?'

'Beautiful. Come down and I'll make pancakes.'

Marek cooked while Safi told Indigo about her latest diving adventures – a moray eel had darted from a crevice, giving her a fright; she had flown over kelp during a drift dive; and she had found a gas mask in the glove box of a Jeep on the deck of a shipwreck. Indigo enjoyed listening to Safi, she got so excited about diving it was infectious. She was describing an unusual fish she had seen on the night dive when she stopped and pointed at something behind Indigo.

'What is that?' She drew back in her seat.

Indigo turned and saw the cockatrice slithering towards him, head held high. 'It's a kind of snake. It's harmless,' he said sheepishly. The cockatrice pushed its way onto his lap, looked at his pancake, and clucked loudly. Indigo put a piece in its beak.

Marek shook his head, 'I'm not sure it's a good idea to feed it at the table.'

Safi eyed the cockatrice disdainfully, then carried on talking about the fish.

As Indigo listened to her, he decided that perhaps Safi and his dad didn't seem concerned about the cockatrice because they saw so many strange creatures under the sea; to them, perhaps the cockatrice was no more unusual than an electric eel, a seahorse, or a manta ray.

When Emerald came home she looked even worse than she had the day before. Her hair was grey with slate dust and her eyelids were bruised and heavy. She collapsed in an armchair while Marek made her tea, but before she got a chance to drink it the phone rang. As she listened her face became as grey as her hair.

She put the phone down and turned to Marek. 'My father is missing,' her voice wavered.

Before anyone got a chance to respond, another boom shook the valley and Emerald shot up. She didn't seem conscious of what she was doing. Marek flicked his wheels and flew towards her. Indigo thought he was going to crash into her, but at the last moment he grabbed her, pulled her onto his lap, and spun his chair around.

'Don't go rushing off again, Emerald. He's not waking up that fast. Let's do this properly.' Marek turned to Safi, 'Pack camping gear for two; roll mats, sleeping bags, stove, and torches.' He turned to Indigo, 'You're going with your mother this evening. Pack water, food, and tea. Go on, both of you, let me talk to your mother.'

It was late afternoon when Indigo and his mother set off. The shadow of the mountains crept slowly across the valley floor. Indigo carried the cockatrice in his rucksack until the village was out of sight, then he lowered it to floor. The cockatrice followed close behind as they walked steadily along the valley, up the fell, and onto the slate topped mountains.

Emerald stopped for a drink of water and offered her bottle to Indigo. 'You know we aren't going to see Mrs Wood, right?'

Indigo nodded. 'I know.' He was thinking about the slate dragon his mother had told him about when he was young. *Could it be real?* The idea was ridiculous. *Or was it?* The last

26

couple of days he had seen a magpie-cat and a giant bat, met the yellow-eyed, ghoulish Dr Orava, and he had a cockatrice slithering at his heels. *Maybe there are such things as dragons.* Indigo's heart beat faster.

They scrambled up a steep rock face covered with loose slate. The sun was about to drop behind the mountains on the other side of the valley when they reached a large cave. Huge slabs of freshly broken slate were littered outside the entrance.

'Is this where the earthquake was?' Indigo peered into the cave.

'I guess you could say this was the epicentre of the disturbance. Are you ready?'

Broken slate crunched under their feet as Emerald led Indigo through the cave. The cockatrice waited outside, peering into the cave with disapproval. Emerald put her hand on the cave wall. 'What do you see, Indigo?'

Indigo studied the wall. It was dark grey slate, shining with a silvery sheen of graphite. There were curved surfaces not typical of slate, and areas of uniform pattern, like overlapping roof tiles. *Scales!* They were scales on a huge convex belly. A wing was folded above it, and a clawed foot beneath it. A long tail disappeared back into the rock.

Air rushed into two large nodules in the slate and the cave wall heaved and swelled. *It was breathing!* The nodules were nostrils, on the end of a huge snout. A closed eyelid loomed above them.

A dragon was embedded in the rock, like a fossil. Indigo put his hand on its belly. It was hard as slate, silky as graphite, and warm. 'It's a dragon,' Indigo whispered. The words jolted him, and the anticipation that had been building since they set off suddenly erupted into feverish excitement.

'IT'S A DRAGON!' Indigo beamed and his eyes lit up. 'It's alive, isn't it?'

Emerald smiled and nodded.

'He's been asleep a long time, nearly twenty years, but he's waking now, working his way out of the rock.'

Sooty, sulphurous air billowed out of the nostrils. Slate scales clattered sonorously. The whole rock face vibrated, and

27

chunks of slate started crashing to the floor.

'Outside!' Emerald shouted, pointing at the cave entrance.

The rock fall didn't last long. Indigo built a small fire while Emerald cooked on a camping stove. After they had eaten they sat by the fire, watching the last of the light in the sky fade away. The cave, and the valley, were quiet. A small group of deer wandered down from the fell top. The cockatrice clucked, and they bolted down the hill, leaping over rocks as they ran.

Indigo sat silently, feeding the fire, waiting for his mother to tell him more about the dragon. She finished her tea and put the kettle on to boil again.

'The dragon is called Graphite,' she began. 'I've known him all my life. He followed me here from Poland, and fell asleep not long after, slowly sinking into the rock.' She turned to the cave, looking concerned. 'I'm not sure he's ready to wake up, Indigo. A large bat has been disturbing him. I don't know if it's attacking him, trying to wake him, or just being nosy.'

'A bat gave me the cockatrice egg.' Indigo stroked the cockatrice, which was curled up against his leg. It hissed affectionately.

Emerald glanced at the cockatrice, 'I've been meaning to ask you about her. I'm sorry, Indigo, I've been so preoccupied.'

'How do you know it's a 'her'?'

'The males have bigger combs.'

Indigo wanted to ask how she knew about cockatrice, but instead he just said, 'Oh.'

'Did you bring your catapult?'

'Yes,' Indigo rummaged in his bag.

'We'll take shifts to keep a lookout, and scare the bat off, shall we?' Emerald yawned and gazed into the fire with tired eyes.

'Get some sleep, Mum. I'll do first watch.'

'Thanks, Indigo.' Emerald fell asleep moments after she zipped up her sleeping bag. The kettle boiled and Indigo made himself tea, even though he didn't usually drink it. It was hot and sweet and a pleasant warm feeling spread from his belly.

Indigo watched the night sky intently, straining to place every noise he heard. It was hours before anything happened, but when it did, it happened incredibly fast.

CHAPTER SIX

THE CATAPULT AND THE BAT

The bat swooped into the cave over Indigo's head, and the walls shook. Rocks fell inside and outside, smashing to the floor. Thick grey smoke billowed from the cave entrance. Emerald shot up and fought with her sleeping bag. She broke free, stamped her feet out of the bag, and ran into the cave.

Indigo fumbled with his catapult and bag of steel bearings. He loaded a bearing in the pouch and stretched the rubber tubing backwards. The bat flew out of the cave. Indigo aimed and fired. The bat spun out of control and landed with a dull thud some distance down the hill.

Indigo stumbled into the cave. He turned on his torch and the beam lit air thick with ash and slate dust. The whole rock face heaved and trembled. Emerald was trying to soothe Graphite, her hand resting between his nostrils. Graphite's claw was thrashing, struggling to escape the rock. It was useless. Too much of him was trapped.

His eye darted under his eyelid, and a fissure shot across the lid with a loud crack. Upper and lower lids split apart, and the lower lid slid down, revealing a huge, black, elliptical pupil that contracted in the beam, unveiling a silver-grey iris.

Emerald turned, shadowing her eyes with her hand. 'The bat?' she shouted.

'I hit it.'

'Find it!'

Indigo paced down the hill, sweeping the ground ahead with the torchlight. He slowed when the beam illuminated the cockatrice. The top half of her body was bolt upright, the bottom half laid in a frozen meander behind her. She was looking down at the motionless bat, triumphant and disapproving. She clucked.

Indigo knelt and examined the bat. How he'd managed to hit it in the dark when it was flying, he didn't know. Good luck, or bad luck?

Footfalls preceded Orava's appearance. His pale face came out of the darkness like a distorted oval moon. He was furious. 'You didn't have to shoot it!' He jabbed a yellow claw in Indigo's direction.

Indigo studied a bloody spot on the bat's head. He reached out and touched its back. It didn't respond.

Orava grabbed Indigo's cheeks with one hand, squashing his face and forcing his mouth open. Pain flared where Orava's icy fingers dug in. Orava leaned forwards and peered into Indigo's mouth. 'Do you have any loose teeth?'

Indigo's arm flew up and batted away Orava's hand. 'Don't touch me!'

Orava lowered himself to the floor on the other side of the bat, and picked it up tenderly. For a moment he looked like he was going to cry. Then Indigo saw his dry, yellow eyes and wondered if he was capable of crying.

'It was attacking Graphite,' Indigo said. It sounded like an excuse. The bat was dead, and he felt guilty.

Orava cradled the bat in his arms, 'It wasn't attacking your dragon.' He folded the bat's wings over its body, 'Where's your satchel?'

'You mean Opi's satchel?'

'Where is it?' Orava snapped.

'I lost it.'

Orava grunted in frustration.

Emerald stormed down the hill. Her red curls were glowing, flying around her head like fire. Her green eyes burned with hatred as she glared at Orava. 'Get away from my son!' she shouted.

Silent green flames appeared from nowhere, licking the air, coiling around Orava's limbs and fingers. They disappeared so fast Indigo was left wondering if they had been real, imagined or illusion.

'Where's my father?' Emerald demanded.

32

Orava rose and looked down at her. 'I don't know,' he said slowly and firmly.

A minute passed. No one spoke or moved. Then Orava nodded his head towards Emerald. 'If you'll excuse me, I must see to this bat.' He strode away, into the darkness.

Indigo looked at his mother out of the corner of his eye; she was staring at the spot where Orava had stood. 'Is Graphite all right?' he asked.

'I think so,' she turned and climbed the hill. 'Why don't you go and check him?'

Indigo went back into the cave. Graphite was asleep, but his claw and wing were twitching. He was running, or flying, or fighting, in his dream. More of his wing was exposed now and an elbow was free, but the wing tip was still stuck in the rock. His tail had broken free completely, and trailed out of the rock face into a pile of broken slate.

Graphite was incredible. A living, breathing, dreaming fossil. Indigo wondered how long it would take the dragon to break free, and what would happen then. A dragon couldn't go unnoticed for long.

The cockatrice was waiting for Indigo at the cave entrance. Indigo stroked her head behind the fleshy comb. Dawn was lighting the fells, although the sun wouldn't rise over the mountains for hours.

Emerald was sitting with her back to the cave, making tea. 'Would you like to go to Poland, Indigo?' She looked at him intently. 'You could stay with Omi until Opi turns up.' Her voice faltered and she breathed in slowly, 'I need to stay here, with Graphite, and your dad and Safi, well, they find life in the mountains hard.'

'OK,' Indigo didn't know what else to say. His head was spinning.

'I hoped you'd say that. I already asked your dad to start making the arrangements,' Emerald smiled. 'I'm not worried about you, Indigo. You're sensible, but I do want to say one thing,' she draped her arm over his shoulder, 'of all the things

33

you've seen, and are going to see, there's just one thing I think you might find difficult to accept, but I want you to know that it's possible.'

'What's possible?'

'You have control over what you become.'

Indigo nodded, wondering what she meant.

'Go on then.' Emerald squeezed his shoulder and gently pushed him away.

Indigo raised his eyebrows, 'What? Now?'

'No time like the present,' she turned away and picked up her mug.

Indigo was reluctant to leave, 'Will you be all right?'

'Of course I will,' she said, and blew on her tea. Just for a moment a green flame danced in the air she breathed out.

Indigo's house was quiet. All the curtains were drawn. He walked past it, and kept walking until he reached the library. The sign on the door read "Closed". He hovered in front of it, wondering whether to knock.

Rue opened the door. 'What are you doing here?'

'I'm looking for Orava,' Indigo followed Rue inside. 'Is he here?'

'No.' Rue heaved the door to the basement open, 'Come on.' She skipped down the stone steps and disappeared behind a bookshelf on the far side of room.

Indigo found her perched on the edge of an oversized armchair, shuffling through papers heaped on a low table.

'Orava has a bat –' Indigo began.

'She's fine.' Rue interrupted, handing him some tattered papers bound with string.

Indigo looked at the writing, 'I can't read Polish.' He passed the papers back to her.

Rue rolled her eyes, 'You'll have to figure it out for yourself then.'

'Figure what out?'

'How to take care of your cockatrice,' Rue craned her neck towards Indigo's rucksack. 'Is it in your bag?'

'Yes,' Indigo nodded.

'Let it out,' Rue ordered as she walked across the room.

Indigo lifted the cockatrice out of his bag. She coiled around his leg nervously. Rue returned with a handful of grain and poured it onto the floor in a neat pile. The cockatrice hissed at her venomously. Rue hissed back even louder. Indigo crouched down and shielded the cockatrice protectively.

The corners of Rue's mouth twitched. 'I won't hurt her.' She returned to the armchair, and the cockatrice slithered up to the grain, pecked it, and clucked. Rue glanced up at Indigo.

'You shouldn't have shot the bat last night.'

'I killed it,' Indigo whispered, looking at his feet.

'I told you, it's fine,' Rue said impatiently, 'Orava has a few dragon's teeth. But that's not the point. What you did was unfair.'

'I was trying to protect the …' Indigo hesitated.

Rue tilted her head and narrowed her eyes. 'Apart from those bewildered indigo eyes, you look like him.'

'Who?'

'Your grandfather. You have his build, and his mannerisms. He had dark curly hair when he was younger too.'

'How do you know?'

Rue ignored the question, 'You even have a gap between your front teeth like him.'

'Well, you have Orava's yellow eyes.' The words fell out of Indigo's mouth.

Rue sat back and tensed her jaw. 'You can go now.'

'I'm sorry,' Indigo picked up the cockatrice, 'I didn't mean …'

'Just go. I've things to do.' Rue's eyes were hostile, but the corners of her mouth raised upwards in the hint of a smile.

CHAPTER SEVEN

THE AMBER PALACE

Indigo had been in the car all day. He was stiff and uncomfortable. Safi's endless diving chatter was irritating him and, worse still, he was annoyed with himself for letting it irritate him. The cockatrice was curled up next to him. She lifted her head and lowered it onto his knee. She understood how he felt.

Marek parked the car and Safi got out. 'I can smell the English Channel,' she breathed in deeply, 'the Atlantic Ocean and the North Sea.' She walked to the back of the car and lifted Marek's chair out. Indigo opened his rucksack and the cockatrice slid inside.

The man behind the booking desk gawped at Marek and Safi. Indigo hadn't left the valley in so long he'd forgotten how much strangers stared at his dad and Safi. They were so pale, and their hair so fair, they looked almost albino; and their skin had an amphibian dampness to it, even when they had been out of the water for a whole day. Indigo looked at the man and felt irritated again. He didn't like the city. He missed the mountains.

They spent the ferry crossing on deck. It was dark when they left, and the lights of the port disappeared into the horizon as they hummed into blackness. Marek wrapped himself in a blanket and fell asleep in his chair. Indigo and Safi sat on a bench, snuggled under the same blanket. Safi fell asleep and Indigo slipped his arm around her, remembering times when they were younger and she had read him stories in bed. The sea air gusted. Indigo tasted salt on his lips, felt it crusting over his skin and hair.

For the next three days they drove along coastal roads, through France, Belgium, the Netherlands, and Germany. The sea was always within sight. Sometimes it was far away, across sand and mudflats alive with birds. At other times it was so close to the road the waves threw spray over the car.

Indigo studied the map, 'Wouldn't it be quicker to drive inland, instead of sticking to the coast?'

Marek laughed, 'Yes, but I love the sea.'

Looking out of his window, Indigo began to realise how little he had seen of the world. Less than a week ago he would have been happy to stay on his fells forever. *How could he have thought that?* There were so many different landscapes waiting to be explored.

Huge areas were covered with fields of crops that made a patchwork of the land in brilliant, unexpected, colours. There were forests similar to the ones in his valley, and forests like nothing he had seen before. Dark, spooky pine forests where towering trees with bare trunks grew close together and there was nothing on the forest floor but dried pine needles and permanent shadow. Indigo caught glimpses of unfamiliar animals – hares, wild boar, and elk, along with glimpses of familiar creatures – deer, rabbits, and squirrels.

They spent their evenings and nights camping on beaches. Safi and Marek swam in the sea while Indigo and the cockatrice picked their way over barnacle encrusted rocks, peering into pools. Marek cooked on open fires and they watched glorious sunsets while they ate. The sky was vast with no mountains in the way, the endless horizon perfectly flat.

On the third day they drove through a small village and along a narrow, sandy track. On one side of the track huge sand dunes towered above them, and on the other side was an inviting beach with golden sand. A few fishing boats lay abandoned, and there was a single beach hut with peeling red paint. The sky was bright and blue.

Safi got out of the car and stretched. 'Isn't it beautiful, Indigo? The Baltic!'

Indigo stood beside her and gazed at the sea. Sunshine

glittered on the gentle waves.

'We'll camp here tonight,' Marek wheeled up next to Indigo. 'Olga will pick you up in the morning. You'll like her, she's been friends with your mother for a long time.'

'What will we do, Dad?' Safi asked.

'Me and you, Safi, will stay here for a while.' Safi jumped up and down in excitement. Marek turned to Indigo. 'Omi and Olga both know how to get in touch with me. I can be with you in a day or two.'

'I'll be fine, Dad.'

'I know,' Marek smiled, 'but remember we're here if you need us.'

Indigo nodded. It was good to know.

Marek looked far out to sea, 'This is where I'm from.'

'You met Mum here, didn't you, Dad?' Safi was taking off her shoes.

'How did you meet her?' Indigo asked.

'She fell in over there,' Marek pointed far across the water. 'I rescued her, brought her to this beach, and we fell madly in love,' he smiled. 'Of course, I'm sure she'd tell it different.'

'The ruins of an amber palace are out there,' Safi said. 'Can we show him?'

'Not today, Safi,' Marek shook his head.

'It's not that far, or that deep,' Safi pleaded.

Marek frowned, 'We didn't bring any diving gear.'

'We can just swim out. He has to see it, Dad, it's so beautiful. Please!' she begged.

'I could try,' Indigo ventured, looking at the excitement in Safi's face.

Marek swam close to Indigo. At first the water was warm, with gentle lapping waves, but further from the shore cold currents hit them, and the waves swelled. Safi swam ahead and dived under, disappearing for minutes at a time. Indigo swam slowly and steadily, but it wasn't long before he was tired and cold.

Safi surfaced. 'Come on,' she urged.

'I think we should go back,' Marek said, 'we can do this another day.'

'But I can see it,' Safi protested. 'Come on, Indigo, come and see.'

Indigo dived down as deep as he could and looked in the direction Safi was swimming. He could see nothing but the dark blue water that surrounded him. He rose to the surface and gasped for air. 'I can't see it.' He struggled against waves that seemed to be fighting with him, and with each other.

'Indigo,' Marek grabbed him under his armpits and pulled him back towards the shore. 'You'll see it another day. I promise.'

The cockatrice was waiting for Indigo on the beach, her head held high, her golden scales shining in the sunlight. Indigo collapsed on the sand and waited for the sun to dry and warm his body. The cockatrice leaned over him and clucked disapprovingly. Indigo stroked her, under her beak.

'I'm sorry,' he said. 'Did I worry you?' The cockatrice curled up and rested her head on his chest.

Marek, Safi, Indigo, and the cockatrice were sat outside the beach hut the next morning when a classic car rolled along the sandy track towards them. The cockatrice darted into Indigo's bag, and he fastened it.

A large lady climbed out of the car and lumbered towards them. Thick, muscular, hairy arms burst from her frilly sleeves. She had long brown hair, thick eyebrows, and a fluffy moustache and beard. She smiled broadly and bent down to hug Marek. Then she turned to Indigo. She slapped his back hard and crushed him in a great hug.

'I'm Olga,' she announced. 'I'll take you to your grandmother.'

They drove all day. The car was slow and uncomfortable. Olga talked merrily, sometimes in English, sometimes in Polish. She laughed at her own jokes, pointed out landmarks, and told stories. She stopped frequently to talk to old men and women leaning on fences or sitting on stoops, watching the world go by. Indigo smiled and nodded, and stared out of his window until he could see nothing but his own reflection.

He was woken by Olga hitting him hard on the shoulder.

'We're stopping here,' Olga pointed to a single white light piercing the blackness ahead. As they approached Indigo saw it was the porch light of a small wooden cottage nestled on the shore of a huge, round lake.

The cottage was empty. Olga muttered to herself in Polish as she made a fire and rummaged in the kitchen cupboards.

'Can I help with anything?' Indigo asked.

'No,' Olga shooed him out of the kitchen, 'I'll cook, you swim.'

A wooden jetty led across the lake. Billions of stars were suspended in the sky, and every one of them reflected in the dark waters. Indigo placed his bag on the end of the jetty and opened it. The cockatrice slithered out, and stared at the lake. She leaned over the water, scooped up a beakful, raised her head, swallowed, and clucked.

Indigo undressed and lowered himself into the water. It was the same temperature as the air, neither warm nor cold. It felt like silk flowing over his skin. He swam out slowly, trying not to disturb the water, then floated in silence. Stars shone above him, below him, all around him. He was in the middle of the universe.

The rain started unexpectedly. Small drops landed gently, creating widening circular ripples. Then the rain fell harder. It splashed into the lake violently, each drop creating a surge of water that flew back up into the air. Water hit Indigo's face from above and below. Soon he could see nothing but the water on his eyelashes and refracted light.

A loud hiss cut through the rain and Indigo turned to the jetty, blinking the water from his eyes. The cockatrice was poised over the lake, as if it were about to strike.

Something touched Indigo's leg. It was cold, slimy, muscular, and strangely prickly. Indigo kicked frantically. Thick towers of water rose out of lake around him, writhing and wobbling, a distorted image of the stars in the sky trembling across them. Indigo was confused. *What was he seeing?* He blinked again, but water splashed into his eyes from all directions. It was impossible to focus.

41

Indigo made an effort to tread water calmly and rhythmically. As he relaxed, his fear ebbed away. He was aware of the presence of a creature, but felt sure he was safe. The stars in the water towers changed colour, flickering orange, blue, and silver. Indigo watched the waves of lights, amazed and enthralled. He was enveloped by a feeling of complete contentment.

The water towers slid back into the lake and bubbles plumed to the surface. Indigo was alone. He stayed in the lake for a long time, willing the creature to return.

The rain stopped, and Olga called him from the cabin. Indigo pulled himself onto the jetty and rose to his feet, feeling refreshed and clean. The sea salt that had coated him for days was gone, and his skin was supple again.

Indigo slept well that night. He dreamed of mountains. Not rolling fells, but huge, towering, jagged mountains that hid dragons and griffins, and strange creatures that could turn their arms into water and stars.

CHAPTER EIGHT

THE FRIENDLY GIANTS AND THE UNICORN

When Indigo first glimpsed the Tatras his heart leapt. The mountains sat high above the horizon and were topped with jagged, snowy peaks. As they drove closer the mountains rose higher until they loomed over him like friendly giants.

The road became steep and winding as they left the last village behind. They zigzagged their way over mountains, each one taller than the last. Indigo had never been on roads this high up. His body lurched from side to side as Olga navigated the twists and turns that took them up, and back down, the peaks. Terrifying sheer drops fell away from the edge of the road. One slip on gravel, one skidding wheel and they would plummet to certain death. Indigo looked down and imagined falling, speeding towards the valley floor, then swooping up and flying off into the wider vista.

As they travelled deeper into the mountains Olga talked less, and Indigo talked more. He asked the names of peaks, rivers, and lakes, he guessed the types of rocks and trees, and he exclaimed in delight when he saw mountain goats, eagles, and wolves. The lakes below were deep blue, bright green, or perfect reflections of the mountains and sky. The lower slopes were covered with forests of spruce and pine, and Indigo wondered what creatures hid in their depths.

Olga's car struggled up a worryingly tilted stretch of road, and stopped.

She pulled up the handbrake, 'We're here.'

Indigo spun around, 'Where does Omi live?'

Olga pointed up a steep grassy slope, 'A cart will probably be waiting. The cabin is on the other side of the plateau.'

'Aren't you coming?'

43

'No,' Olga turned to Indigo and he was surprised to see her frowning, her eyes welling with tears. 'You, your parents, and your grandparents think it's nice and beautiful and wonderful in these mountains, but I know different. You be careful, Indigo.'

Indigo didn't know what to say. Olga had been so cheerful throughout the journey, it disturbed him to see her like this.

'My son was stolen by these mountains,' Olga pulled a lace handkerchief out of her sleeve and dabbed her eyes.

Indigo was horrified, 'Stolen? How old was he? Is he?'

'He's about your age now. Thirteen?'

Indigo nodded.

'He was nine when it happened. He was stolen by a beast, an evil creature. These mountains are full of them,' Olga looked at the mountains with disgust, 'and now your grandfather ...' Tears rolled unchecked down her hairy cheeks.

Indigo was relieved when Olga left the car. She hugged him tight, and waved him off, all the while muttering things in Polish and sobbing.

Indigo walked up the grassy slope. He took a zigzag path, as the car had done. It was the only way to gain height safely. When the road was out of sight he released the cockatrice. She glided through the grass, hissing, happy to be free of the bag. Every few steps Indigo turned and took in the view. It was breathtaking. He had never been this high before. He was sure if the highest peak in the Lake District were put here, it would look like an anthill.

Despite the astonishing scale of the Tatras, there were plenty of things that made Indigo feel at home. The granite peaks, the clusters of larch trees, and the bending foxgloves were all familiar friends.

Indigo was hot and sweaty when he reached the plateau. It was covered with tall grasses and wild flowers swaying in the breeze. Outcrops of purple heather and grey boulders rose above the plants.

A wagon lay ahead. It was similar to the cowboy wagons in Wild West movies, but smaller. It had low wicker sides and an arched metal frame supporting a canvas cover. The wheels were big, with knobbly off-road tyres.

Indigo held up his hand, signalling the cockatrice to stay back, and walked towards the horse hitched at the front of the wagon. The horse was tall, slender, and completely black. He approached it from the side.

'Hey there, fellow,' he said softly and the horse turned its head. A long, pointed, perfectly black horn protruded from the centre of its forehead. Indigo's jaw dropped in wonder.

'You are beautiful.'

He lifted a hand to the unicorn's nose. The unicorn breathed, and warm air flowed between Indigo's fingers. Indigo stroked its neck and scratched behind its ears, admiring the soft black coat and shining, spiralling horn.

The cockatrice slithered forwards, and the unicorn whinnied. 'It's all right, she's harmless,' Indigo reassured. The unicorn tossed his head and started to walk across the plateau. Indigo walked alongside, and the cockatrice meandered behind. Every so often the unicorn stopped and flicked his head, as if beckoning Indigo to get into the wagon, but Indigo didn't want to ride in the wagon – he was enjoying the company of the unicorn, and the view.

The sun sank low, the peaks glowed red and dark shadows engulfed the valleys below. At the end of the plateau the mountain rose up again, steep and rocky, into the sky. The summit was lost in cloud. Snow melted into watery crevices that carved their way down the mountain, hinting at hidden waterfalls and caves. Indigo stopped, in awe of the mountain, and heard Omi shout his name. She was standing on the porch of a small log cabin nestled at the base of the cliffs. Indigo followed the unicorn to the cabin, feeling nervous. It had only just occurred to him there was no one to translate.

Omi was short and round. She wore a long black skirt and a red shawl. Her eyes were cloudy with old age, and deep folds of wrinkled skin curved around her face. Her grey hair was pulled back in tight, straight lines. She grabbed Indigo's hand and squeezed it tight. 'Indigo, Indigo, Indigo,' she smiled, revealing toothless gums. She held his hand for a long time, smiling, chuckling, and repeating his name. Indigo's face started to ache from smiling back.

When she released Indigo she turned to the unicorn, and spoke to him tenderly as she unbuckled the harness. The unicorn followed her to the side of the cabin, where she drew a bucket of water from a well. She left the unicorn drinking, and ushered Indigo to a rocking chair on the porch.

Indigo took off his rucksack and sat down. The cockatrice coiled around his leg. Omi babbled something in Polish and shuffled inside the cabin. She returned with a bowl of water for the cockatrice, and a tall glass of a cloudy drink for Indigo.

'Thank you,' Indigo said. It tasted cold and spicy.

'*Dziekuje*,' Omi said, slowly and loudly, as if Indigo might be deaf.

'Jen-koo-yeh,' Indigo tried to repeat what she had said.

Omi folded over and laughed. She carried on chuckling as she placed a few carrots in a large wooden bowl on the porch steps, and sat in a rocking chair next to Indigo. She pulled a long pipe from her skirt pocket and packed it with sweet smelling tobacco. The unicorn appeared from the side of the cabin with a shining wet muzzle, walked to the bowl of carrots, and started eating noisily.

'Onyx.' Omi pointed her pipe at the unicorn.

'Onyx. Is that his name?'

Omi nodded. She lit a match, puffed on her pipe, and gazed at the jagged pink peaks in the distance. The unicorn finished eating, raised his head high, and licked his lips. Indigo went to him and stroked his face and neck. The unicorn blew air out of his nose, nudged Indigo gently, then walked away towards a thick spruce forest that dropped away from the side of the plateau. Indigo watched him disappear into the trees.

Omi lowered her pipe. 'Olga,' she said, and mimed driving a car.

Indigo nodded, 'Olga drove me here.'

Omi rubbed her fists in front of her eyes and pretended to cry.

Indigo nodded again, 'Yes, Olga cried.'

Omi rose, smoothed the front of an imaginary dress, and dabbed her eyes with an imaginary handkerchief. It was a fair impression of Olga. She laughed and babbled something in Polish.

Indigo felt uncomfortable. Olga had driven him all the way across Poland, her son had been stolen by the mountains, yet Omi was making fun of her. He looked at Omi, laughing and rocking in her chair, and decided he had to let it go. She was old.

The shadow of the mountain crept across the plateau. Omi pointed at things and named them in Polish, loudly and clearly – the peaks, the sky, clouds, trees, flowers, birds, and everyday items on the porch. Indigo repeated the words. Omi laughed every time he spoke. She laughed harder and harder, rocking in her chair, tears streaming down her wrinkled cheeks.

Omi showed no sign of going indoors as the evening drew on and darkness slowly enveloped them. When the stars appeared and the air grew cool Indigo pointed to the cabin. Omi shook her head and pointed to the sky. 'Smok,' she said. 'Smok Wawelski.' She pointed her finger down – she was staying where she was.

Indigo went inside and brought out a blanket for her. Then he made tea. He carried it out on a tray along with some food he had found on a marble slab in the kitchen – some soft cheese, bread, and cold sausage.

Omi put her hand over her heart, like his mother did when he did something nice for her. She babbled something softly and finished it off with, 'Indigo, Indigo, Indigo.' She ate and drank and smoked some more, chuckling softly and repeating Indigo's name. Before she fell asleep she pointed at Indigo, and pointed at the sky again. 'Smok,' she said, 'Smok Wawelski.' Then she rocked herself to sleep and snored loudly.

Indigo watched the sky darken and the stars brighten. It was incredible here, more beautiful than he had ever imagined, but he had an uneasy feeling. He didn't know what he was supposed to be doing. He stepped off the porch and turned around. The silhouette of the mountain towered over the cabin.

'*Sanktuarium*,' Omi shouted from the porch.

Indigo pointed at the mountain. '*Sanktuarium*,' he repeated, 'is that what the mountain is called?'

'*Sanktuarium*.' Omi didn't laugh.

Indigo suddenly had the feeling that the mountain would play a large part in his future here

CHAPTER NINE

THE LONG GOODBYE AT THE COCKATRICE CAVES

Indigo was woken by voices raised in anger. For a moment he couldn't remember where he was, then as the cool mountain air hit his lungs he realised the chair he'd slept in could rock and he remembered.

He recognised Omi's voice, then Rue's. They were arguing hard and fast in Polish, inside the cabin. Indigo rose and the cockatrice slid off his lap. He admired the view, stretched, and walked into the cabin. Omi and Rue were out of sight in the back kitchen. Wary of interrupting their argument, Indigo lingered in the living room.

Four large paintings in rough wooden frames hung on the far wall. One was of his mother. She was young and smiling, sitting amongst wildflowers with a daisy chain crown on top of her enormous red hair. The next painting was of a young boy with big grey eyes, and curly red hair like his mother's, playing in a mountain stream. Indigo wondered who it was. The boy looked so much like his mother he could be her brother – but she had never mentioned a brother. There was also a painting of a fierce red dragon flying towards an orange sunset, and the last painting showed a grey dragon, curled like a cat, asleep in a slate cave.

Indigo spotted two ornate silver frames on a sideboard, and he leaned over to study them. The first held a painting of Omi and Opi on their wedding day, holding hands in front of a stone castle. They were almost unrecognisable. Omi was a fairy-tale princess, elegant and slender, with flowing golden curls. Opi was tall and slim with curly dark hair. Indigo saw the resemblance to himself, but decided the gap between Opi's front teeth was much wider than his. The second frame held a photograph of a modern day Omi and Opi, outside their cabin. Omi was less wrinkled and her eyes less cloudy, but the photo couldn't have been taken that long ago. Opi was as Indigo remembered him from his last visit – tall, skinny, with shining eyes, and a halo of frizzy white hair and beard.

The argument in the kitchen escalated. Indigo braced himself and walked in. Omi and Rue stopped and stared at him.

'Your grandmother is being unreasonable,' Rue folded her arms over her chest. Before Indigo could ask her why, Omi flew into a tirade in Polish, all of it directed at Rue. Omi ended the outburst with a flourishing arm gesture and a frown. Rue turned to Indigo. 'She says I'm the one being unreasonable.' Omi erupted again – she shouted, jabbed her finger at Rue and stamped her feet. Rue shouted back. Soon they were both yelling at each other, over each other, neither listening to what the other had to say. Indigo didn't understand a word of it. He stood bemused as the argument reached a crescendo, then subsided into a bad-tempered silence.

'She says I can take you to the cockatrice caves after your breakfast,' Rue informed Indigo as she strode out of the kitchen, 'to release your cockatrice.'

Indigo's heart missed a beat and his hands became cold and clammy. He didn't *want* to release his cockatrice. Omi passed him a tray of breakfast things, cradled his cheek in her hand, and muttered something in Polish. Indigo understood the sentiment behind the words – if he loved the cockatrice, he had to let her go.

They ate on the porch. Omi rocked her chair in quick, short movements, watching Rue out of the corner of her eye suspiciously. After breakfast Indigo packed some things into a small rucksack, assuming he would be out for most of the day. Before they left, Omi gave Rue strict instructions, and babbled something softly to Indigo that he didn't understand.

They skirted the vertical face behind the cabin until they came to a jagged crag where grassy patches grew between huge cracked rocks. They climbed upwards, meandering between boulders, staying on grass wherever they could.

The sun was high in the sky when they reached a tall, vertical face. When Rue disappeared into the cliff Indigo realised it was split. There was a narrow path between the two sides. The path was in shadow, the air cool and refreshing, and Indigo heard the unmistakable sound of a waterfall.

The corridor opened to reveal a tiny paradise – a pale green pool, enclosed by lush green vegetation and surrounded by high cliffs. A waterfall tumbled into the far side of the pool, and a permanent rainbow hovered in the spray.

Indigo gazed at the scene, mesmerised by its beauty. Soon he became aware of the cockatrice. Cockatrice were everywhere – hiding in vegetation, swimming in the water, coiled in cracks and crevices in the cliff face. There were small ones, like his cockatrice, and big ones, twice that size. Some had enormous floppy red combs, and Indigo realised they must be the males. A few clucks rose above the sound of the waterfall, and more cockatrice joined the chorus, until a cacophony of clucks echoed up the cliffs.

Rue sat at the water's edge and took off her shoes. Indigo did the same. Indigo's cockatrice looked at them both disapprovingly, clucked, and slithered off, around the edge of the pool, behind the waterfall, and was gone.

Rue dangled her feet into the water, 'I don't like long goodbyes either.'

Indigo stared at the waterfall, grief and rejection sinking in his chest. *Was that it? Would he see her again?* He tried to console himself with the thought that the cockatrice would be happier with her own kind. It didn't help, he missed her already. 'Is the entrance to the cockatrice caves behind the waterfall?' he asked Rue.

'That's more of exit, but the caves are there, inside the *sanktuarium.*'

'Is that what the mountain is called?'

'*Sanktuarium,*' Rue looked at him like he was stupid, 'means sanctuary. Why can't you speak Polish?'

Indigo ignored her question, 'So the cockatrice here are safe?'

Rue nodded. 'Trained weasels collect the eggs from all over

51

the Tatras and take them to a secure cave deeper in the mountain. When the cockatrice hatch they have to swim through a pool of Rue Water to reach the cave behind that waterfall.'

'Who trains the weasels?'

'Orava trained the first ones, but now they train each other. It's a self-sustaining system.' She raised her head proudly. 'There hasn't been a cockatrice-related death in the Tatras for over three hundred years.'

'Are you saying Orava is more than three hundred years old?'

'Your grandfather is even older.'

'How is that possible?'

'For Orava, or your grandfather?'

Indigo leaned back on his hands. He didn't want to hear anything about his grandfather from Rue. He could talk to Opi when he came back.

'Orava's not all bad, you know.' Rue looked at Indigo with narrowed eyes. 'He's good with animals, and he never liked the idea of a creature with a death-darting gaze slithering into Krakow. That's why he did this,' Rue nodded to the waterfall.

Indigo was confused. 'I guess it was a good thing for him to do.'

'Your grandfather didn't see it that way. He didn't like Orava meddling in his sanctuary. They had a big fight over it, and never spoke again. Not that they were friendly before.'

'I thought you said Orava set up the sanctuary?'

'The cockatrice caves are a tiny part of the sanctuary. Orava is responsible for them, but the rest of the sanctuary is your grandfather's doing.'

Indigo put on his shoes, 'Will you show me?'

Rue shook her head, 'I've never been inside. Your grandfather didn't allow me, or Orava, into his precious sanctuary.' She looked up at the cliffs. 'I know someone who might show you around though, if you like.'

CHAPTER TEN

WOJTEK THE YETI

Indigo hesitated before leaving the cockatrice pool. He glanced around, searching for his cockatrice, willing her to follow him, but she didn't. He kept looking back as he curled higher up the mountain, but gave up after a while. His cockatrice wasn't coming.

Rue led him up a steep, rocky slope. They had to use their hands to stay balanced and pull themselves upwards. Eventually they climbed over a crest and reached a plateau where they could walk unaided. Ahead, the mountain rose up again in impossible, sheer cliffs striped with snow. A smooth, white, lenticular cloud sat on the peak like a conical hat, obscuring it from view.

Rue pointed to a dark area at the base of the cliffs.

'That's Ruby's cave.'

'Who's Ruby?' Indigo shielded the sun from his eyes to get a clearer view. The whole plateau was a scree slope that seemed to spill out of Ruby's cave.

'Another dragon,' Rue headed for the cave. 'She's not in.'

'Where is she?'

'How should I know? Maybe the same place as your grandfather.'

It was difficult to walk. Boulders, cobbles, pebbles, and gravel moved underfoot and threw Indigo off balance with every step. Closer to the cave air drifted out, warm and dry. It burned the back of Indigo's throat. He closed his mouth and peered inside. The floor and walls were black with soot.

Rue turned away from the cave and skirted the base of the cliff.

'Aren't we going in?' Indigo hovered at the cave entrance.

'I told you I've never been in the sanctuary, and if I were to go in, that's not the entrance I would –' Rue was cut short by a loud cackle, followed by a growl. They both looked up. The magpie-cat was on a ledge above the cave. It tilted its head, stared at Indigo, then pecked at one of its cat paws. It was lying on something faded, brown, and leathery. A brass buckle glinted in the sunshine. *Opi's satchel!* The magpie-cat stopped pecking its foot and chattered angrily. Rue walked away.

'Rue, wait!'

'If you climb up, it'll fly off.'

'But it's got my grandfather's bag.'

'And I'm sure it will return it to your grandfather, if he ever comes back.' She carried on walking.

A lump rose in Indigo's throat. *If.* He studied the cliff, and failed to see a single hand or foot hold that could get him up to the ledge. He looked at the magpie-cat again, nestled on Opi's bag, then followed Rue.

The ground fell away steeply at the edge of the plateau. They descended over crispy grass and moss, reached a chasm, and scrambled down into a damp and shady spruce forest. Rue led Indigo slowly and silently towards a low, dark cliff hidden behind a thick cluster of trees. An unpleasant musty smell, with a hint of ammonia, wafted out of an arched cave in the cliff. Rue crouched to the side of the cave entrance and pressed her fingers to her lips.

'Wojtek,' she whispered.

A shuffling noise came from inside the cave, and a human silhouette emerged, as tall as Indigo, but broader, and massively muscled. The creature stepped into the light. He was covered in a thick coat of long, fluffy, brown hair, and was wearing knee-length shorts. His face, hairy and scowling, turned to them and Indigo saw the resemblance straight away.

'You're Olga's son!' Indigo exclaimed.

'Shhhh!' Wojtek and Rue both glared at him.

'Don't mention Olga,' Rue whispered to Indigo, 'he had an argument with his mother over whether or not they were Yetis, and he's very sensitive about it all.'

Wojtek shoved Rue's shoulder and whispered at her fiercely,

for a long time. Rue tilted her head from side to side impatiently and rolled her eyes. 'Wojtek wants me to tell you he's a dangerous Yeti, and you have to be careful around him. But he's not a Yeti and he's not dangerous. He's just a sad, deluded boy.'

Indigo looked at Wojtek. He was very big, and very hairy. 'How do you know he's not a Yeti?' he asked Rue.

'He doesn't look anything like a Yeti, and neither does his mother. He's just a hairy human. He probably has a condition, like hypertrichosis.'

Rue turned and whispered to Wojtek. He whispered back. Soon they were whispering hard and fast, teetering on the brink of an argument. Indigo heard the name 'Smok', at which point Wojtek slapped him hard on the back, and carried on whispering to Rue.

Rue nudged Indigo. 'Wojtek says he's been taking care of the sanctuary for your grandfather.' She whispered to Wojtek again and he shook his head. Rue folded her arms over her chest and frowned. 'He won't let me come in the caves, but he'll take you, as long as you do what he says, and be careful not the wake the Yetis. The *real* Yetis,' she added venomously.

Wojtek grabbed Indigo by the arm and pulled him into the cave. Wojtek was very strong, and Indigo wondered if he really was a Yeti. He decided it didn't matter what he believed – it only mattered what Wojtek believed.

The smell of ammonia grew stronger. Indigo put his hand over his nose and followed Wojtek deeper into the cave. The floor was covered in stiff, dry grasses that crunched as they crept over them. A loud snore drifted across the cave and Indigo wondered what the other Yetis looked like, and how many of them there were.

Wojtek put a finger to his lips, raised himself onto his hairy toes, and led Indigo silently to the back of the cave. They turned sharply, and walked along a dark corridor breached by shafts of sunlight descending from holes in the rock ceiling. The corridor split, Wojtek pointed to the left fork, flapped his arms and made a chatter-growl. Indigo nodded. Perhaps the magpie-cat had a cave in that direction. They took the right fork and walked steeply downwards.

Wojtek stopped frequently, pointed to other shafts and tunnels, and made strange noises – shrieks, whistles, barks, roars, hisses, and croaks. He moved his fingers and arms to show writhing, clawing, stalking, scuttling, creeping, and jumping. Indigo couldn't imagine what creatures he was trying to describe, and wished Wojtek would just show him.

At the entrance to a low, wide tunnel Wojtek growled and hissed, and parted the hair on his upper arm to show Indigo a thick, jagged scar. He told the story of his injury in Polish, using flamboyant gestures. Indigo couldn't work out what creature had scarred Wojtek, but he managed to figure out it was Opi who had stitched him up afterwards.

They headed deep into the mountain. The air became icy, and the ceiling shafts less frequent. They were plunged into darkness for minutes at a time. Indigo was cold and beginning to feel lost and vulnerable in the maze of tunnels and caves.

A warm breeze hit Indigo and he tasted salt on his lips. Wojtek stopped abruptly and Indigo took a step forward, so that he stood next to him. The corridor ended.

They were high in the wall of an enormous cavern overlooking a huge underground lake. On the other side of the cavern was an elliptical hole in the roof. Sunshine poured through the hole, and landed on a beach – an underground beach, on the edge of an underground lake. Gentle waves sloshed onto coarse grey sand. Indigo had never seen anything like it, anywhere, not even in books. He was astounded.

Indigo followed Wojtek along a narrow path cut into the cavern wall, which led down to the beach. Wojtek walked across the sand and stood at the water's edge, letting the waves lap at his big, hairy feet. He held his arms out and beamed, as if he had created the cavern, and the lake, just for Indigo to admire.

'Wow,' Indigo smiled and nodded.

Wojtek crouched down and beckoned Indigo over. He dipped his finger in the water, put it in his mouth, and nodded Indigo do the same. Indigo tasted the water. 'Salt,' he said, surprised.

'*Sol*,' Wojtek pointed to the cavern wall. The pale grey rock

56

was patterned with convoluted white lines.

Indigo's head whipped around as a huge plume of bubbles erupted in the middle of lake. Wojtek laughed and pointed to a shadowy mound lurking below the surface.

'Indigo, kraken.'

CHAPTER ELEVEN

THE KRAKEN

A bow wave rushed towards them, ahead of a shadowy mound. The mound stopped abruptly and sank, and the wave washed onto the grey, sandy shore. Indigo held his breath as a tentacle curled out of the water. It was enormous, as thick as a tree trunk, with suckers the size of saucers, but that wasn't the most striking thing about it. Its skin was hypnotic, alive with light and colour, perfectly mimicking the ripples and dapples of the water.

The tentacle coiled around Wojtek's waist. He made no attempt to move away or fight it off. Slowly Wojtek was lifted up until his hairy feet were dangling above the water. He laughed and slapped the tentacle hard. Waves of orange and yellow light flashed along the tentacle as it lowered him gently down, uncoiled, and slid back into the water. Wojtek ran back to the cavern wall and disappeared into a dark narrow tunnel.

Indigo stepped into the water. It seeped through his trousers and trickled into his boots, but he was focused entirely on the shadowy mound just beneath the surface. The kraken slipped the top of its head out of the water. Silvery eyes with dark crescent-shaped pupils protruded from its bulbous head, and rotated towards Indigo. A tentacle rose, like a tower of water. It reached for Indigo, its translucent skin flickering in a kaleidoscope of blues and greens. Indigo raised his hand, and touched the tentacle. It was cold, slimy, rough, and prickly. The tentacle wrapped around Indigo's arm tightly and pulled him towards the water. Indigo laughed.

'*Krab!*' Wojtek shouted from across the beach. The kraken released Indigo, and glided backwards. It floated at the surface, its silver eyes fixed on Wojtek, who was carrying a crab twice the size of a dinner plate, its pincers waving angrily ahead of him. With a grunt of effort, Wojtek threw the crab across the water and the kraken dived down after it, leaving a trail of bubbles in its wake. Wojtek beamed at Indigo. 'Kraken!' he shouted. '*Kraken jesc Krab*!'

The erratic waves resulting from the kraken's dive dissipated into a gentle, regular lapping, and the lake became calm again. Indigo followed Wojtek across the beach and up the cavern wall, to the elliptical hole in the roof. The wall was steep but craggy, with plenty of good foot and hand holds. Wojtek pulled himself up, over the lip of the hole, and disappeared outside. Indigo climbed the last few metres, and poked his head out.

A sheer vertical face dropped away, plunging to a grassy plateau below. Omi's cabin was beneath them, smoke rising from the chimney. Wojtek pulled Indigo up onto a precarious ledge, and thrust a rope into his hands. Indigo realised what he was going to have to do, and his hands became sweaty. He thought of falling, accelerating down to the ground, and he thought of flying. Both thoughts made him nervous. He clung to the rope tightly, focused on climbing down one step at a time, and relaxed as he approached the plateau. When his feet touched the grass he was with dizzy with exhilaration. He let go of the rope and looked up. There was no sign of the hole, the cavern, or Wojtek. The rope slid up the cliff face and Indigo realised Wojtek wasn't coming down.

A tray of food was waiting for Indigo. Omi was gently rocking in her chair, smoking her pipe. She leaned forward as Indigo stepped onto the porch and flashed a gummy smile, her cloudy eyes gleaming.

'*Sanktuarium*?'

Indigo nodded.

Omi babbled something in Polish and laughed. 'Wojtek?' she asked.

Indigo nodded again, 'Yes, I met Wojtek.'

Omi rose, puffed her chest out and pulled her shoulders back. 'Wojtek,' she barked. 'Yeti.' She laughed uncontrollably, sat down and wiped the tears from her cheeks. Her laughter subsided and she took a puff on her pipe. Her eyes lit up again and she lurched forward. 'Kraken?' she asked eagerly.

Indigo smiled. He had met the kraken.

They ate and drank. Omi rocked and laughed. The sunset lit the peaks, and darkness fell. Omi fell asleep in her chair, and Indigo covered her with a blanket. He was lost in his thoughts, staring at the stars, when Omi's breathing became laboured. He looked across at her and it struck him how old and fragile she was. There was no smile on her lips, no light in her closed eyes, and her wrinkles lay heavy on her face. He slid a log under her chair to recline it. Her breathing improved for a while, but she started wheezing again. Her eyes opened in panic and her hand went over her heart. Indigo picked up her other hand and looked into her eyes, but she didn't see him. She was struggling to catch her breath. Indigo had never felt so helpless. *What could he do?*

Indigo spun around when he heard a noise, not far from the cabin, something heavy stumbling on grass. He peered into the darkness. 'Who's there?' he shouted.

Omi wheezed, and squeezed his hand so tightly it hurt. He turned back to her, crouched down, and put his hand on her shoulder. He hummed a lullaby, one his mother had sung when he was young. Slowly her breathing returned to normal, her eyes closed again, and she fell back into sleep. When her hand finally relaxed, Indigo left the porch and crept to where the noise had come from, straining his eyes to make sense of what he could see in the starlight – a clump of grass, a rock, and *a pair of dark shoes*.

Indigo lifted his head to see Orava's pale face and angry yellow eyes. Orava's hand shot out and grabbed Indigo by the neck. His claws dug into the soft skin below Indigo's ears. Indigo fought for breath as he was lifted from the floor.

'*Where is your grandfather?*' Everything about Orava was furious. Indigo made a strangled sound and Orava dropped him. He fell to the floor, put his hand to his neck, took a deep breath, and looked up at Orava. His dark hair was dishevelled, his gnarled fingers splayed. Orava leaned forwards and whispered into Indigo's ear, 'If you don't find him, Wanda will die.' Indigo felt cold, scared, and confused. He closed his eyes, willing Orava to go away, and when he opened them again, Orava was gone.

Indigo didn't sleep much that night, and when he did it was an uncomfortable sleep in which he dreamed of Omi. She was the fairy-tale princess from her wedding picture, reaching out to him, unable to breathe, while Dr Orava watched her with his cold, yellow eyes.

Indigo woke with a start.

Wojtek was leaning over him, holding what could only be described as a Cyclops marmot with a really bad case of conjunctivitis.

CHAPTER TWELVE

THE CYCLOPS MARMOT

Indigo had only seen marmots in books. The creature would have looked strange to him even without the single eye in the middle of its forehead, glued shut with gloopy yellow stuff. It resembled a squirrel, but it was enormous – at least two feet long – and had small, rounded ears and a twitchy, rabbity nose.

Wojtek was holding the marmot under its armpits and its flabby shoulders rolled over his hands. Its mouth had drooped open, revealing two long, thin, gnawing teeth on its upper and lower jaws. It had thick, soft fur in shades of brown and grey.

'*Cyklop Swistak*!' Wojtek announced and pushed the creature even closer to Indigo's face.

The marmot's eye was now right in front of Indigo, and he could see all too clearly how swollen and sore it was. The eyelids were firmly stuck together with a mixture of sticky and crusty pus. Indigo recoiled.

Omi came out of the cabin, waving her arms and jabbering at Wojtek. She took the marmot and put it in her rocking chair. It sat bolt upright, its paws clasped together in front of it, as if it were waiting for something. Omi returned with a bowl of water, some cotton wool, and a basket. She gave the basket to Wojtek and he bounded off the porch and started collecting grasses and flowers. Then she turned to Indigo and said loudly and slowly, '*Ksiazka. Opi ksiazka.*' She opened her hands like a book. Indigo went into the cabin to get Opi's book from his bag.

When Indigo returned, the marmot was on Omi's lap, and she was gently swabbing its eye with wet cotton wool. He flicked through the pages until he came to a picture of a swollen eye coated in pus. There were other pictures on the page – a

63

daisy-like flower with a yellow centre and white petals, a plant with feathery leaves and tiny yellow flowers, and a picture of a bee. At the bottom of the page there was a recipe, and a picture of a bottle with a round yellow lid. He showed the picture to Omi.

'*Tornister, Opi tornister*,' she said slowly, and slid her hand down an imaginary strap across her body, to an imaginary satchel at her hip.

Indigo shook his head and made the chatter-growl of the magpie-cat as he mimed it flapping away. Omi nodded and chuckled, wrapped her arms around the marmot's waist, and rocked it back and forth. It made a soft chattering sound.

Wojtek jumped onto the porch with the basket full of grasses and flowers. He crouched down in front of the marmot and passed it stalks and stems. The marmot took the offerings with its front paws and nibbled at them delicately.

Omi babbled to Wojtek while he fed the marmot. Indigo recognised his name, plus '*sanktuarium*', and the word *szpital*, which he knew meant hospital or infirmary. When they finished talking Wojtek pointed to the mountain towering behind them.

'Wojtek, Indigo, *sanktuarium*,' he said proudly, and then pointed to the picture of the bottle with the round yellow lid. Indigo nodded.

Wojtek lolloped up the mountain like a Yeti. He moved so fast Indigo found it hard to keep up. By the time they reached the cracked face that led to the waterfall and the cockatrice caves Indigo was hot, sweaty, and thirsty. He would have loved to stop and rest by the green pool and see his cockatrice again. He wondered if she missed him, if she would slither over and cluck at him. But Wojtek bounded straight past the cracked face and continued up the mountain.

They scrambled up the steeper section, crossed the scree plateau, and arrived at Ruby's cave. Wojtek disappeared into the darkness. Indigo followed him to the back of the cave, sulphurous air burning his nostrils. On his left was a huge mound of gravel with a crater in the centre of it, presumably where Ruby nuzzled into bed. Something glistened amongst the gravel and Indigo wondered if Ruby hoarded gold, like storybook dragons. At its darkest point the cave narrowed and turned sharply, and they entered a corridor lit by shafts, similar to the one behind Wojtek's cave.

Wojtek stopped and pointed out two holes in the rock floor, no bigger than his hand. He mimicked a whiskery weasel face with his own whiskery face, then made a clucking sound, like a cockatrice. Indigo nodded. They were weasel tunnels, leading to the cockatrice caves.

Wojtek continued down the tunnel until it split. He pointed to the left fork, which headed downwards, and said 'Yeti' while pointing at himself. Indigo nodded again. That fork must lead to Wojtek's cave. They took the right fork, passed several more junctions, and started to climb steeply. Indigo was thinking they must be near the top of the mountain when the corridor widened, opening into a large airy cave. Light streamed through a large hole in the sloping rock ceiling. A huge, chunky, wooden table filled the cave. It was strewn with papers, notebooks, bottles, vials, syringes, tweezers, spoons, bowls, tins, dried leaves, and limp flower heads. Cupboards and drawers lined one of the cave walls, and were topped with small cages and boxes.

'*Szpital*,' Wojtek announced, '*Opi szpital*.' It was Opi's infirmary.

There was a scuffle, and a weasel jumped off the table and pattered away with a small yellow vial in its mouth. Wojtek shouted as he ran after it, but it was too fast for him. He turned, shouting and waving his arms at Indigo. Indigo tried to figure out what he was saying. He decided Wojtek was trying to tell him the weasels kept stealing things, but he wasn't sure. He kept nodding until Wojtek finished talking, then they both began examining the bottles and vials on the table.

'Ha!' Wojtek held up a small brown bottle with a round yellow lid. Indigo walked over and patted him on his hairy back. Wojtek beckoned him towards an opening in the cave wall. On the other side was an even larger cave. A thick sheet of clear plastic covered a hole in the cave wall. The sky on the other side of the makeshift window was white. They were in the middle of the cloud at the top of the mountain. The air was

warm and humid, like a greenhouse, and the cave was filled
with plants. Herbs, flowers, berries, and leaves in a myriad of
shapes and colours sprouted from long wooden troughs. Wojtek
walked along the troughs, naming the plants and stroking them
gently. He arrived at one plant and mimed a stomach ache, at
another he mimed backache, and at another he coughed. He was
demonstrating what the plants could be used for – they were
medicinal plants.

It was dusk when they returned to the cabin. Indigo loved this
time of day. It was cool and calm, the air was thick with yellow
light. Tiny insects danced among the tall grasses and flowers,
and the peaks of the High Tatras glowed in the distance. As
they approached the cabin the Cyclops marmot, now sat upright
on the porch steps, beat its tail and chattered its teeth. Indigo
crouched down and talked to it softly, telling it about the
medicine he had brought. It sat back on its haunches,
accentuating its fat blond belly. Indigo opened the bottle. An
eye dropper was inside. Omi shouted '*Dwa*' from the porch,
and Indigo carefully placed two drops in the marmot's eye.
    Omi passed Wojtek a small bundle wrapped in a cloth. He
grabbed it, waved, and lolloped away. Indigo sat in the rocking
chair next to Omi and she passed him a glass of the spicy,
cloudy drink. It cooled his head and warmed his belly. He put
his glass down, and noticed Opi's book on the table. The golden
edge of it was shining and he remembered something. He
picked up the book and folded it gently. There *was* a picture on
the page edges – a hidden picture that was only revealed when
the pages were fanned. It showed a castle on a green hill. A
fairy-tale princess with flowing golden curls stood on a balcony
in the castle tower, and in a cave under the castle was a dragon,
a sleeping white dragon. Walking towards the cave was a man,
carrying a sheep on his shoulders.
    Omi leaned over, pointed to the princess in the picture, and
pointed at herself. '*Ja*,' she said, 'Wanda.' She smiled wistfully.
She was the princess. Her finger moved to the dragon, 'Smok,'
she said firmly. She pointed at the man carrying the sheep,
'Orava,' she said. Lastly, she pointed at the sheep. 'Boom,' she

whispered and splayed all her fingers in an imaginary explosion.

The marmot whistled, and a huge bat swooped over the cabin. Indigo smiled; it was the first time he had seen Orava's bat since he shot it. He was pleased to see it flying again. Omi leaned back in her chair, puffed her pipe, and gazed at the peaks. Her cloudy eyes looked into the past, and for the first time in his life, Indigo wished he could speak Polish. They watched the glowing peaks fade to grey shadows, then to black silhouettes.

Indigo dreamed of Opi. He was standing by the door of his cabin, smiling behind his fuzzy, white beard, exposing the gap between his two front teeth. Omi appeared behind him, wiping her hands on her apron, and Opi bent down and kissed her on the cheek. Then with a couple of strides of his long legs he was outside Ruby's cave, carrying a sheep on his shoulders. The sheep was struggling and bleating desperately.

A deep rumbling reverberated the air. A dozen boulders exploded out of the cave mouth, and a flash of red lightning whipped after the rocks. There was a crash and another rumble as the rocks hit the scree and caused a minor avalanche. The cliffs quivered. A subterranean growl swelled to a roar, and the cliffs shook. The crescendo became painful. Indigo tried to ride the wave of thunder but it was pulling him from his sleep. His organs were vibrating, and his ear drums felt like they were about to rupture. When he thought it couldn't get any louder, he woke up. The silence was overwhelming. Then the rumbling began again. A deep rumbling was coming from the sanctuary, making the ground shake.

CHAPTER THIRTEEN

HYDRA VS. KRAKEN

Wojtek hurtled out of the darkness, running towards the cabin and shouting urgently. He was scared, angry, and breathless. Omi pulled Indigo from his chair and pushed him off the porch. Before he had a chance to register what was happening, Indigo found himself running after Wojtek towards the vertical cliffs behind the cabin.

When they reached the cliffs, Wojtek passed Indigo the rope and grunted impatiently. Indigo climbed, pulling himself up, hand over hand, and walking his feet up the face. Every few steps a boom came from above, and thunder rolled inside the mountain, sending shockwaves down the cliff face.

As Indigo approached the entrance to the kraken cavern he could make out individual noises – rocks smashing against rocks, thumping onto sand, and splashing into water. Chilling siren screams pierced the air, discordantly overlapping each other. Indigo swung his body into the cavern and climbed down the cliff, stealing glances at the scene in between searching for hand and foot holds. The right cavern wall was collapsing into the lake in great chunks. Something on the other side of the wall was hitting it with immense force. It was big, angry, and it was trying to break through.

Wojtek caught up with Indigo on the beach. He pulled two large handkerchiefs from his shorts, passed one to Indigo, and tied the other over his face, covering his mouth. Indigo did the same. He led Indigo across the beach and into the narrow tunnel in what was left of the cavern wall.

They emerged in a dark, wet cave. The siren noises became unbearable, and even through the handkerchief Indigo could smell an overpoweringly sweet, pungent stench. The floor was wet and slippery. When the next crash vibrated through the cave both Indigo and Wojtek skidded to the floor. Wojtek remained on all fours and crawled towards the sound. Indigo followed. As his eyes adjusted to the dark he saw thick stalagmites rising from wet pools, and equally thick stalactites clinging to the ceiling.

The floor of the cave became swampy. Indigo couldn't feel rock anymore, only wet slime that was getting deeper. He rose to his feet and saw a pale beam of light falling from the ceiling. A porthole to the sky was framing the constellation Hercules. An ear piercing scream rent the air, followed by an almighty bang.

A massive serpentine body contorted in the shadows ahead of them, splattering mud through the air and sending shockwaves through the slime. Fangs were everywhere, long and pointed, dripping from wide, gaping mouths that were hissing and spitting. Rounded heads darted up and down, back and forth, controlled by a tangle of necks that converged on to the same snake body. Indigo's eyes widened as he recognised the Hydra.

There was a flash of movement near one of the Hydra's heads, and Indigo spotted the bat, weaving between its twisting necks. A Hydra head screamed and lurched after it. The bat swooped away and the head missed and smacked the wall instead, sending rocks crashing into the swamp. Indigo and Wojtek watched helpless as the bat continued to dash around the cave. It flew erratically, confused and panicked, seeking an escape route. Its movements sent the Hydra into a frenzy, in which every head, and its tail, were whipping after the bat, missing it, and thumping the cavern wall instead. The whole cave was in danger of collapse.

The wall took another hit which triggered a major rock fall. The Hydra recoiled its heads as huge boulders splashed into the swamp on one side and the lake on the other, creating a hole that grew larger as more boulders fell. The swamp was now connected to the lake, and water rushed from one side to the other.

A metallic, maniacal laugh echoed around the cave and Indigo turned to see Orava, a dark silhouette in a small pool of starlight.

'The cavern is collapsing!' Indigo shouted.

Orava stopped laughing and the cave fell quiet. 'Will your grandfather come and save his precious sanctuary now?' he sneered.

'He's not here!' Indigo yelled.

'Then let it collapse!' Orava laughed again, but there was pain and anger in his twisted expression. The sirens started up again, drowning out Orava's laugh.

Huge wet tentacles shot across the hole in the cavern wall and slapped around the hydra's necks. They closed their grip and coiled tighter, pulling the Hydra heads down, and across the swampy cave floor. The Hydra struggled frantically, pulling back and stretching the kraken's tentacles. The kraken and the Hydra became a dark, writhing, sinuous mass of tentacles, necks, scales, and suckers. The kraken was stronger. The Hydra was slowly being dragged, screaming, into the lake. A single Hydra head lifted and smashed into what was left of the wall above the kraken. Rocks rained down on both the kraken and the Hydra, and the whole mountain shook. Stalactites fell and smashed to pieces all around the cave.

When the rocks stopped falling the cave was forebodingly silent. Indigo, Wojtek and Orava stood frozen. Indigo moved first. He walked towards the mound of boulders where the kraken and the Hydra had last been seen. Wojtek and Orava followed.

The Hydra was motionless, its necks sprawling limp among the boulders. Where the necks converged on to the snake body a huge stalactite had fallen and pierced the scales. Indigo and Orava moved towards the wound, stepping over rocks and necks in their path.

'What have you done?' The words burst out of Indigo's mouth.

'What have I done?' Orava was angry again. His yellow eyes flashed and he jabbed a finger towards Indigo's chest. 'I didn't bring it here. This ...' he pointed at the Hydra, '... is not

71

meant to be here. That ...' he pointed to the lake on the other side of the rubble, 'is not meant to be here either. This place is dangerous. It was dangerous when your grandfather was here, and it's going to be apocalyptic without him. There are too many beasts in one place, and they don't belong here.' He turned his back on Indigo and bent over the Hydra's wound.

Wojtek stumbled over boulders to the lake, crouched down, and peered into the dark waters. There was no sign of the kraken. He splashed gently, rhythmically, with his hands. There was no response from the lake. Wojtek turned to Indigo, his eyes wet, his mouth open in disbelief, and dived into the lake.

Indigo turned to the Hydra. Orava was pulling the stalagmite from its body. 'Is there anything we can do?' Indigo asked.

'I need dragon's teeth,' Orava snapped. 'I have three. I need six more.'

Wojtek pulled himself out of the water and walked towards them, shaking his head and waving a hand in front of his eyes. It was too dark for him to see anything under the water. Orava said something to him in Polish, and he ran off. Indigo sat on a boulder. Orava stood tall over the lifeless Hydra, but he looked defeated.

Wojtek returned with a pestle and mortar, six long pointed teeth, and thick rubber gloves. Orava ground the first tooth and put the powder into his cupped hand. His long fingers awkwardly overlapped each other as he tried to close them over the powder. He walked to the nearest Hydra head and said something to Wojtek. Wojtek put on the gloves, grabbed hold of the top jaw, and grunted as he lifted it up with one hand. Sharp translucent fangs fell forwards, dripping with a clear sticky liquid. A sweet, pungent smell cloyed Indigo's nostrils. Wojtek used his other hand to pick up the narrow forked tongue and hold it to one side as Orava dropped the powder under it. Wojtek moved the tongue back into place and closed the jaw.

Orava, Wojtek, and Indigo worked together in silence as they treated all the Hydra heads. When the task was complete they sat a small distance away. 'How long will it take?' Indigo asked. Orava didn't answer. Minutes passed and nothing happened. Then the Hydra started to move. One head rose, then fell. Another yawned, and another hissed, its tongue darting out and licking the air. Slowly it came to life, as if it were waking from a deep sleep. When all the heads had lifted from the floor it glided into the darkest corner of the swampy cave and curled up.

Indigo turned around. Orava was nowhere to be seen. Wojtek had moved closer to the lake and was looking out across its dark, gently lapping waters.

'Kraken,' he said anxiously.

Indigo put his hand on Wojtek's hairy shoulder. 'I think I know someone who can help.' Wojtek must have understood from the tone of Indigo's voice, because he smiled and led the way back to the cabin.

CHAPTER FOURTEEN

THE TROUBLE WITH DRAGONS

The cliff face glowed orange in the dawn light. Indigo and Wojtek cast long shadows as they climbed down. Omi was waiting for them on the porch, surrounded by baskets and platters of food – freshly baked bread, smoked cheese, spiced sausages, and cake. She grabbed their cheeks and landed gummy kisses where she could.

Wojtek was bombarded with questions as he filled his hairy arms with food and sat on the porch steps. While he ate he told Omi what had happened, using a great deal of gesturing and sound effects. Emotions grew and faded on Omi's face as she listened – horror, tension, anger, relief, and finally, concern. She turned to Indigo when Wojtek had finished. 'Marek?' she asked, eyebrows raised. Indigo nodded, relieved she had the same thought as him – his father might be able to help the kraken.

Omi shuffled into the cabin and returned with a thin silver whistle. No noise came out when she blew it, but after a few minutes a large bird winged its way to the cabin. The magpie-cat fluttered straight into Omi's arms and started purring. Omi stroked it from the feathers behind its head to the tip of its furry tail, muttering to it softly. She reached into her pocket and pulled out an orange ring and a metal tool, and with a quick deft movement she attached the ring to one of the magpie-cat's bird feet. Then she whispered 'Marek' close to its head, threw her arms in the air, and the magpie-cat flapped away.

Omi smiled and settled back into her chair. Wojtek laid on the grass, holding his belly, and fell asleep. Indigo watched the sunrise lighting the peaks. They rose from a thick layer of cloud, and gradually turned from dark silhouettes to embers alive with light and shadow.

Indigo's blinks lengthened, and he slowly drifted into sleep. He dreamed of Opi again. He was outside Ruby's cave. The cliffs had stopped shaking, the rumbling had subsided, but Opi was tense, his eyes closed. The soft clatter of scales moved towards him and hot, dry breath hit his face. Opi opened his eyes to a thick sooty cloud. The smell of sulphur burned the back of his throat. His heart missed a beat as he realised how close Ruby was. Her eyes, like burning coals, were right in front of his, scorching him. Blood red scales dripped down her face, gleaming in the light emanating from her eyes. She grinned menacingly, exposing enormous white teeth like sharpened buffalo horns. Opi reached his hand towards her, but she rose onto her hind legs until she towered above him. She opened her wings, plunging Opi into shadow, then lifted her head towards the sky and breathed a plume of fire into the atmosphere. She was magnificent. A mass of muscle, armour, tooth, and claw.

Indigo woke feeling restless. He left Omi sleeping in the shade of the porch, and walked to the sanctuary. He saw Wojtek climbing the rope up the steep face, and decided to take the longer route up the mountain. Lost in thought Indigo soon found himself by the cracked face leading to the cockatrice caves. He walked down the cool corridor towards the waterfall, and saw Rue sitting by the green pool. A weasel ran up to her, and she took a small yellow vial from its mouth, and gave it something in return, which it ate before running off again.

'Do you get them to steal things for you?' Indigo walked over and sat next to her.

'If someone needed medicine would you stop them getting it?' Rue glared at him defiantly.

'Of course not,' Indigo said. 'Who needs medicine?'

Cluck! A cockatrice darted out from behind the waterfall and rushed towards Indigo, its head raised high and its body whipping behind in urgent curls. It didn't stop until its big red eyes were inches away from Indigo's face. Indigo smiled and stroked her under her beak. She clucked softly, leaned forwards, and rested her cheek on his. It felt cold and rough. Indigo understood how she felt. She had missed him after all. She sank into Indigo's lap in a neat coil. Indigo put his hand on her back and felt complete.

The cockatrice was bigger than the last time he saw her. Her scales shone a brighter gold, and her eyes, comb, and beak were redder. On her back were two small, white, feathery bumps.

'She's growing wings.' Rue pointed to the bumps. 'Not many do that. It's quite rare. They'll have to be clipped.'

Indigo put his arm over the cockatrice protectively.

'Why?'

Rue looked at him like he was stupid. 'So she doesn't fly off and start a colony somewhere else.' She rose to her feet. 'I've got to go, and I would imagine you have things to do.'

Indigo nodded, but as she walked away he called after her, 'I'm going to check on Wojtek and the kraken. Do you want to come?'

'You'll need me to translate,' Rue said.

'If you say so,' Indigo smiled. The cockatrice slid off his lap, looked from him to Rue, and back again, clucked disapprovingly, and slithered off behind the waterfall.

'Come on,' Rue said. 'You'll see her again.'

Indigo led Rue up the mountain, to Ruby's cave. The air in the cave hit him hard, burning his throat and making him tense as he remembered the Ruby from his dream – the scorching eyes, the blood red scales, the menacing grin, and enormous teeth. He hurried through the cave and along the maze of corridors, and surprised himself by reaching the kraken cavern without taking a single wrong turn.

From their vantage point, high in the wall of the cavern, bright sunlight streamed through the hole in the roof and Indigo could see the extent of the damage from the night before. A massive part of the left cavern wall had collapsed, revealing the swampy cave on the other side. Most of the boulders were gone, sunk to the bottom of the lake, but a few littered the beach.

'It's beautiful,' Rue whispered. They followed the path down the cavern wall to the beach. 'So there is a kraken in there?' She scanned the water.

Something breached the surface near the collapsed wall and gasped for air. It was Wojtek. He took a few deep breaths and dived back under.

'There was. After last night I don't know if it's alive or dead.' Indigo looked at Rue out of the corner of his eye. He wondered how much she knew about what had happened, and he wondered whose side she was on – or if there were any sides to be on at all.

It was as if Rue read his mind. 'I told you before, he's not all bad. Orava is trying to protect people.'

'I think I'm beginning to understand that,' Indigo agreed reluctantly. 'But why is he so angry?'

Rue sat and pushed her fingers into the sand. 'He grew up in Krakow, when the city was young. It was beautiful. Cobblestone streets, wooden buildings, roofs painted gold and blue, willows drooping into the clear blue waters of the River Vistula, and a stone castle on a green hill overlooking it all. The people were peaceful and happy.' She turned to Indigo and her eyes darkened with anger. 'That was before Smok came.'

'The dragon?' Indigo sat next to her, and she continued.

'Krakow never recovered from the damage he did. Dragons can be so destructive.' Rue shook her head. 'Over time the smoke cleared, the ash washed away, houses were rebuilt, crops grew back, livestock recovered, and trade returned. But it wasn't the same. Every family had lost a loved one, either killed by Smok, or by the starvation he caused. The people changed from peaceful to warlike. They built armies and weapons. They were scared, suspicious, and selfish, thinking only of self-preservation. Orava was a tailor. He made beautiful clothes for the king and the princess. Smok turned him into a killer.'

'Orava killed Smok?' Indigo felt a pang of grief. He had thought Smok was alive – Omi kept pointing to the sky and saying his name, as if she were waiting for him.

Rue nodded. 'Orava filled a sheepskin with explosives, sewed it up, and planted it near Smok's cave.'

'Boom,' Indigo whispered, remembering the picture on the side of Opi's book.

'Orava never forgave Smok for making him do that, or for what he did to the town. He's still angry about it, and the anger eats away at him.' Rue looked at Wojtek, who was now swimming towards them. 'So you see he has good reason to hate him. To hate all dragons.'

Wojtek waded out of the water and started shouting at Rue. With his hair wet and stuck to his body he looked smaller and thinner, more like a boy than a Yeti. Rue shouted back, and in an instant they were in front of one another, yelling, pointing, stamping, and getting redder. Indigo had never seen Rue's pale face flushed. It made her look different, more alive, but her yellow eyes were chillingly familiar. When she was angry, her eyes looked just like Orava's. The argument continued, and even when they stopped shouting they stood with their fists clenched, snapping. Indigo couldn't understand why they were so angry with each other. 'How's the kraken?' he ventured, looking at Wojtek.

Wojtek looked from Indigo to Rue, frowned, and shook his head. Indigo suspected the look had nothing to do with the kraken. He spoke fast in Polish, and as he kept glancing at Rue it became clear he expected her to translate. Rue talked over him in English, 'The kraken is trapped under rocks, deeper down than he can dive. He thinks it's alive.'

Indigo nodded. 'My father is coming. He'll be able to help.'

Rue translated, and Wojtek disappeared into the tunnel that led to the swampy cave, muttering something about crabs.

The light was fading when Indigo and Rue climbed down the rope, to the plateau. Wojtek stayed in the cavern, to be with the kraken, and Rue disappeared without saying goodbye before Indigo reached the cabin.

Omi was asleep on the porch, and to Indigo she seemed a hundred years older than she had done just a few hours before. She looked shrunken, thinner, and her clothes were baggy. The veins and tendons in her hands stood proud and her cheeks were hollow. Worst of all was her breathing. It was weak and irregular.

Indigo busied himself tidying, cleaning, and checking on

79

Omi every few minutes. He kept hearing Orava's voice in his head. *'If you don't find him, Wanda will die.'* He felt helpless. He was no closer to finding Opi than he had been when he arrived. Indigo thought hard, trying to figure out where Opi might be. He felt a sudden surge of anger towards Opi, and in that moment he understood Orava better. It was Opi he didn't understand. *Why had he set up the sanctuary? Why did he leave?* He had abandoned Omi, who might be dying. He had left the sanctuary to fall apart, and left him in confusion, unable to do anything to help. Indigo sat down and put his fingers to his head, as if it might stop the thoughts from spinning inside his brain.

When Indigo finally slept that night he dreamed he was on a cliff, holding on to a rope, looking down at a log cabin. Smoke curled from the chimney and took the form of a huge white dragon. Omi walked out of the cabin, as the fairy-tale princess in her wedding picture. The smoky dragon floated away, and she grew older. The rope slipped through Indigo's fingers and he fell, faster and faster towards the plateau floor ... until he was caught by the giant gnarled fingers of Orava.

CHAPTER FIFTEEN

THE GOLD TOOTH

Indigo was woken by Omi shouting at Orava. They were both on the plateau, not far from the cabin. She barely came up to his armpit, but she was advancing on him, and he was retreating. She was formidable and fierce. Orava didn't stand a chance. He was holding something out to her as he walked backwards. She grabbed it from his hand, threw it to the floor, and stamped on it, then grabbed his warped yellow fingers and shook them in front of his face.

Indigo jogged towards them, pausing when he noticed the smashed yellow vial on the floor. Yellow liquid was seeping into the ground, the colour of Orava's eyes.

Orava saw Indigo approaching and opened his mouth to say something, but Omi shouted louder and faster. She ended her tirade with a dramatic flourish and a vicious, derisive look. Then she turned and stomped back to the cabin, grabbing Indigo by the shoulder on the way and pulling him behind her. Astonished by her strength, Indigo allowed himself to be pulled along as he glanced back. Orava had sunk to his knees, his face wrought with despair. It was similar to the look he'd worn when the bat had been shot, but magnified a thousand times. Now Indigo knew Orava *was* capable of crying.

A thought occurred to Indigo, a realisation that lifted some of his confusion. *Orava loves Omi.* Orava, the young tailor who saved Krakow from the evil dragon, was in love with the beautiful princess Wanda. In a world of fairy-tales he should have won her hand in marriage for his act of bravery, and lived happily ever after. But she didn't marry him. She married Opi, and he left her alone next to a mountain full of monsters. For

Orava, this was all about Wanda. He still loved her, and was still trying to save her.

Omi sat in her chair and rocked frantically, grumbling to herself and hurling insults in Orava's direction as he walked away. Indigo went inside and made tea. He was coming out of the cabin with a tray when he saw Rue running towards him, out of breath and flustered.

'It's Wojtek, Indigo, please come quickly, he's doing something really stupid!'

Indigo had run in fell races back home, but he had never seen anyone go up a mountain as fast as Rue that morning. He found it impossible to keep up with her, and she kept stopping and ordering him to speed up. It was a relief when they left the rocky mountains and plateau exposed to the sun, and dropped into the cool of the shady spruce forest that hid Wojtek's cave.

Rue led Indigo swiftly and silently through the musty cave, into the corridor behind it, and turned left at the first fork. They had been following the corridor for a few minutes when a noise drifted towards them. Quiet at first, it swelled to deafening proportions. It was the sound of hundreds of birds screeching, shrieking, and cackling, and hundreds of cats meowing, hissing and growling, all mixed together in a maddening, demented symphony.

The cave that opened from the corridor was narrow, but had the highest ceiling Indigo had ever seen. He could barely make out the roof above him. The walls of the cave were deeply craggy and alive with nesting bird-cats of all varieties – magpie-cats, crow-cats, duck-cats, and owl-cats. As Indigo gazed at the colony he recognised other bird-mammal combinations – sparrow-mice, pheasant-rabbits, eagle-foxes, and vulture-wolves.

'Up there!' Rue shouted.

Indigo spotted Wojtek, high on the cave wall, climbing even higher. Angry bird-cats were screaming and flying at him, and each time he lifted an arm to defend himself it threw him dangerously off balance. 'What's he doing?'

'Trying to get your grandfather's satchel.'

'Oh no!'

Wojtek looked down at them, and raised a hand to wave. A magpie-cat took the opportunity to dive at his ribs. It stabbed him hard with its beak and Wojtek winced in pain, tried to cover the wound, lost his balance, slipped, and fell ...

He plummeted to the ground amidst a flurry of feathers and fur, screams and caterwauls, and landed with a sickening, deadening thump.

Indigo ran and knelt beside him. Wojtek's eyes were open but glazed over, and a thin stream of blood trickled from his mouth into his furry beard. Indigo felt for a pulse, but couldn't find one He turned to Rue.

Her fist flew towards him, hitting him hard and square on the jaw. His head reeled sideways and blood spurted out of his mouth. Tears welled in his eyes. He saw sparks and heard a high pitched ringing. Then his whole mouth and jaw started to throb, ache, and swell. He raised his hand to his bloody mouth and looked at Rue in confusion. He tried to say something but only managed a low groan.

Rue scrambled on the floor beside him, picked up a tiny piece of gravel caked with blood, wiped it on her skirt, and disappeared out of sight. Indigo heard a crunching, grinding noise. Rue returned and squashed Wojtek's mouth open. She pushed his tongue to one side with a finger and dropped something under it.

Indigo realised what she was doing. 'My tooth!' he tried to say, but 'Ai oof!' was all that came out of his swollen mouth.

Rue sat back and studied Indigo's face. 'I'm sorry,' she said.

Indigo stared at Wojtek. No more than a minute passed, but it felt like an eternity. Then Wojtek spluttered and rolled onto his side with a groan.

Back at the cabin Omi wrapped Wojtek in a blanket and sat him in her chair with a bowl of cabbage soup. She sat Indigo in the other chair and gave him a cold, damp cloth, which he held to his jaw. And she shouted at Rue. Rue shouted back, but Indigo could tell her heart wasn't in it. After a relatively short altercation she climbed down the porch steps. Omi went into the cabin, and Rue turned to Indigo. 'She's cross because she didn't

83

want me to know about you. She's scared I'll tell Orava. But I won't. I'm your friend, Indigo, remember that. But she's right about Orava, he would kill you if he knew.'

Indigo watched her leave. After she had gone he noticed that Opi's book, which had been on the porch table, was gone.

Omi came bustling out of the cabin beaming. She was carrying a small wooden pot and a bottle with a hexagonal purple lid. She opened the pot. It was full of glistening gold nuggets in different shapes and sizes.

'Aaaaah,' Omi opened her mouth wide. Indigo copied, and she set to work picking out a nugget of the right dimensions. She nodded in approval when she found one she was content with, and opened the bottle. She sprayed its contents into the hole in Indigo's gum. It was freezing, tasted of synthetic bananas, and immediately made the area completely numb. Omi pushed the gold nugget deep into Indigo's gum. It didn't hurt, but Indigo felt the pushing sensation right into his skull.

Omi smiled and nodded Indigo to do the same. An awkward, swollen, lopsided grin spread across his face. Omi chuckled, and danced back into the cabin with her pot. She called for Indigo when she was inside.

He found her looking at her wedding picture. She pointed to the fairy-tale princess, and to herself, 'Wanda,' she said. Indigo nodded. He knew she was the princess. She pointed at Opi. 'Smok,' she said.

'Smok?' Indigo repeated. 'Opi is Smok? Opi is a dragon? *My grandfather is a dragon?*'

'Boom,' Omi whispered. 'Smok. Opi.' She clasped her hands over her heart. '*Smok kotcha Wanda.*'

'Smok loves you, Opi loves you,' Indigo nodded again.

Omi smiled and held up three fingers, '*Trzy jajka.*'

'Three? What?' Indigo didn't understand.

Omi disappeared into the kitchen and came back with three eggs.

'Three eggs?'

She nodded, pointed to the painting of his mother on the wall, and held up one finger. '*Emerald jaj.*'

'My mum was an Emerald egg?' Indigo raised his eyebrows.

Omi pointed to the painting of the red dragon and held up two fingers. '*Ruby jaj.*'

Indigo understood. 'Ruby is your daughter too.'

Omi put one hand on the painting of the boy with red, curly hair, and her other hand on the painting of the grey dragon. '*Graphite jaj.*'

'Graphite is your son. He was a boy, and now he's a dragon.' Indigo suddenly felt cold.

Omi put hand over Indigo's heart and leaned close. '*Indigo jaj,*' she smiled.

The afternoon and evening were peaceful on the porch. Wojtek ate and dozed. Omi smoked and looked at the sky. Indigo watched the light and shadows shifting on the peaks in the distance. He was trying not to think about the events of the day and their implications. He wanted to live in the moment, to soak in the views and the sounds and the atmosphere, so it would become a part of him he could retreat into if ever he needed it and it wasn't there.

Indigo dreamed of Opi and Ruby again that night. Opi was in the shadow of her wings as she breathed a plume of fire into the air. The flames subsided and Ruby looked down. Her eyes still burned, but they were melancholy now. She lowered her head to Opi's, and when he reached for her this time she remained still. He ran his hand over her scales. Each one was as big as his palm. Opi suspended his other hand gently above her nostrils. Ruby closed her eyes and breathed deeply. Opi moved his face closer to hers and they were at complete peace, complete understanding.

A sheep bleated, breaking the silence. Ruby turned and surged towards it in a rush of air. She grabbed it in her massive talons and instantly the sheep was silent. Then the sheep was gone. Ruby swallowed. She glanced back at Opi then starting to run down the mountain, wings outstretched.

She took off, rose high into the air, circled overhead, and disappeared into the distance. Ruby was all dragon. Opi knew what she needed, what she yearned for. The company of other dragons. And he knew how to give it to her.

CHAPTER SIXTEEN

MERMAIDS AND YETIS

Omi, Wojtek, and Indigo were eating breakfast donuts when the magpie-cat fluttered into Omi's lap. She stroked it and broke off a piece of donut, which it grabbed and swallowed whole. Omi took a tool out of her apron pocket, removed the orange ring from its leg, and threw the creature into the air. 'Marek,' she smiled as the magpie-cat flew away. She pushed Indigo and Wojtek off the porch ahead of her. 'Onyx!' she shouted, and whistled loudly. The unicorn trotted out of forest, picking up speed as he crossed the plateau. When he reached the cabin Omi stroked him, and took him for a drink at the well, before harnessing him to the wagon.

Indigo and Wojtek walked alongside the unicorn, across the plateau. They found Safi and Olga struggling to push Marek's chair up the steep grassy slope not far from the road. Olga saw Wojtek, let go of the chair, and put her hands to her mouth and started wailing uncontrollably. Indigo ran to his father and grabbed his chair before it fell backwards. Olga tried to run to Wojtek, but because of the steepness of the slope, and her considerable proportions, it was more of a waddle. Wojtek looked like he was about to run away, but then allowed his mother to crush him in a hairy hug. She sobbed and stroked his fur until he could take no more and struggled free, gasping for air.

Marek and Safi rode in the wagon, while Indigo, Wojtek, and Olga walked alongside. By the time they reached the cabin Wojtek had clearly had enough of his mother, and kept batting her hands away as she tried to stroke and embrace him.

Omi hugged Marek and Safi in turn, for a long time each,

chanting their names. She passed around tall glasses of the cloudy drink, and there was a great deal of babbling, laughing, and smiling. When the excitement settled Marek turned to Indigo and winked. 'So, are you going to show us to this friend of yours who needs help?'

Getting Marek up the steep rock face to the kraken cavern was easier than Indigo thought it would be. They helped him wheel his chair to the base of the cliff, and when he reached the rope he simply pulled himself up with his strong arms and carried on, up the face, hand over hand, legs swaying beneath him. Wojtek, relaxed now he was away from Olga's fussing, displayed his muscles proudly, to compliment Marek's strength. Indigo climbed up after his father, followed by Safi and Wojtek.

Marek reached the beach with only a little help from Indigo and Wojtek. He was exhilarated and excited, and Indigo wondered whether it was from the climb or the promise of the lake. Marek's eyes shone when he neared the water, and Indigo had his answer. They carried him across the sand, waded into the water, and released him. He rolled, dived, and glided away, his legs flowing behind him like a tail.

Safi dived into the water after Marek, leaving a thin trail of bubbles in her wake as she headed to the centre of the lake. Indigo and Wojtek sat on the sand and looked across the water, both wondering what was happening beneath the gently rocking waves.

Marek surfaced and talked to Wojtek, who nodded and bounded off up the cavern wall. Marek turned to Indigo, 'We need rope and muscle to move some boulders, but once we've done that I think the kraken will be fine.' He smiled, 'It's an incredible creature, beautiful.'

Wojtek returned with the rope and the muscle. Four enormous, hairy, brown bipeds followed him down the path in the cavern wall. They were tall and broad, with the confident upright stature of a man, but the fat, muscular proportions of a bear. They had Neanderthal brows, deep set human eyes, large hairy ears, and a long bear snout. Their eyes, ears, and walk gave them a human quality, but overall they were more bear-like.

The Yetis shuffled nervously on the beach while Wojtek and Marek talked. They avoided eye contact with Indigo, stared at Wojtek, huffed air out of their wet, black noses, and moaned. One of them kept clacking its teeth and scratching its belly.

Wojtek threw Marek one end of a rope, and carried the other end to the Yetis. He arranged them using grunts and gestures, and soon they were stood in a line, holding the rope with fat, clawed hands.

Safi surfaced and shouted. Wojtek and the Yetis started pulling. They grunted and moaned as the rope strained. A deep rumbling emanated from the lake, followed by a plume of bubbles breaking the surface. Wojtek and the Yetis dropped the rope and everyone stood silent.

Safi's head rose, and lifted higher until her whole body could be seen. A thick band of water wrapped around her waist, and fell flowing into the lake. It took Indigo a moment to realise it was a tentacle of the kraken, camouflaged as the lake, holding Safi above the waves. She shrieked in delight as the tentacle launched her across the lake and she landed with a graceful dive.

Marek surfaced and swam towards the shore like a dolphin, breaching the waves in graceful curves. He talked to Wojtek while Indigo caught tantalising glimpses of tentacles, suckers, wet silvery eyes, and flashes of light and colour.

Wojtek grunted to the Yetis and they headed up the wall path without looking back. Marek swam closer to Indigo. 'It's free and it's fine. But it needs to return to the Baltic.'

'How?' Indigo couldn't see how that was possible.

'Underwater tunnels lead from here all the way to the Baltic. They link to lakes all over Poland too.' Marek smiled. 'The kraken told me he met you in Olga's lake.'

Indigo thought back to his swim at Olga's. It made sense now. Of course the towers of water in the lake had been the kraken.

'Your sister and I swam here from the Baltic yesterday, through the tunnels, but the entrance to this lake was blocked by boulders. We had to go back to Olga's and travel the last bit by car. Now the path is clear, we'll go back this way with the kraken.'

'Is the kraken all right?' Indigo asked.

'One of his tentacles is torn, but it will recover. Once he gets to the Baltic my family will take care him.'

'Are you a mermaid, Dad?'

Marek laughed. 'I just love the sea.'

Indigo was about to press him for a straight answer when Safi surfaced.

'Have you heard from Mum?' Indigo asked.

Marek nodded. 'We talked to her on the phone two days ago. She's fine.'

'And Graphite?'

'Awake and nearly free of the rock.' Marek looked at Indigo intently.

Indigo frowned, 'What will happen when he breaks free?'

'I don't know, maybe he will come back here.' Marek bit his lower lip, 'What about you?'

'What about me?'

Marek smiled. 'I'm sure we'll see you soon, Indigo.' He didn't look sure.

Indigo splashed into the water and hugged his father, blinking away tears. Marek held him tight. 'I'm proud of you, Indigo, and I love you. That won't change, no matter what.'

'Come on, Dad, let's go.' Safi landed a wet kiss on Indigo's cheek, 'See you soon, Indigo.'

'See you,' Indigo watched his father and sister disappear under the surface. He tried to imagine the journey ahead of them, swimming through dark tunnels with a giant kraken. He wondered how big the tunnels were, and how much the lights that flickered in the kraken's skin would illuminate the darkness underwater. He wondered what other creatures inhabited the tunnels.

'Indigo?' Wojtek broke the silence.

Indigo waded out of the water, and they headed back to the cabin.

Wojtek refused to leave with Olga. She pleaded and shouted and wailed, but he was resolute in his decision to remain a Yeti.

Eventually she gave up trying, Wojtek left for his cave, and she rode away in the wagon.

Indigo and Omi sat on the porch. After Olga and Wojtek's argument, the silence was like a warm blanket. Omi soon fell asleep, and Indigo wandered across the plateau. He felt restless and melancholy. A gentle breeze swished among the grasses. Rue stood ahead of him, holding Opi's book. He reached out to take it and curved and crooked gold writing luminesced on the front. *Okkup Bezzesss.* Indigo silently read the words and understood what they meant. *First Aid for Monsters.*

'Is that Polish?' Indigo pointed to the words.

Rue shook her head. 'No, only some of it is in Polish.'

'What language is it?'

Rue looked at him closely. 'Dragon,' she said. 'Do you understand it?'

'I didn't before.' Indigo looked at the words again. 'Did you find what you were looking for?'

Rue looked away.

'What were you looking for?' Indigo pressed.

'Some hope, I guess.' Rue's yellow eyes were cold and emotionless.

Indigo leaned towards her, 'Are you going to explain anything to me, or just play cryptic games like Orava?'

Rue's eyes flashed with anger, 'I don't want to become like Orava.'

'I've heard we control what we become.' Indigo sat on the grass.

Rue sank down next to him. 'That's not always true. Orava had no choice.'

'Why not?'

'After he killed Smok he expected to marry the princess, your grandmother. He loved her.'

'I figured that out.'

'Clever you,' Rue mocked. 'He was furious with your grandfather, appearing from nowhere and whisking his love away. Twisted by jealously he followed them here, plotting to win her back, or get revenge.'

'What happened to him?'

91

'He found a cockatrice – or a cockatrice found him, depending how you look at it. He was killed instantly. They have a death-darting gaze, you know.'

'Yes, I heard,' Indigo smiled.

'Your grandfather found Orava and brought him back to life with a medicine he'd been working on. Maybe he felt guilty about what had happened, or maybe he was just doing a good deed. Either way, it wasn't the best thing he could have done for Orava.'

'But he saved his life,' Indigo protested.

'At a cost,' Rue brushed the tops of the long grass with her fingertips. 'Orava has to keep taking the medicine to stay alive, and it has some nasty side effects. It's twisted him, inside and out.'

'Maybe you aren't meant to take it for three hundred years?' Indigo suggested.

'True,' Rue nodded. 'He kept taking it to stay with Wanda, and Wanda kept on living. It didn't take him centuries to realise your grandparents were living a lot longer than normal people.'

'He figured out my grandfather is Smok, the dragon.'

'I'm surprised it took you so long to figure out.'

Indigo looked into her yellow eyes. 'How long have you been taking the medicine?'

Rue stood up and walked away.

Indigo shouted after her, 'I'll help you find another cure,' but she didn't look back.

CHAPTER SEVENTEEN

COMINGS AND GOINGS

Indigo woke before dawn the next morning. Omi was rocking in her chair, humming softly. She looked tired and old. Her cloudy eyes were wet, and a tear was working its way down between the wrinkles on her cheek.

Beyond the plateau, dark peaks rose out of an ocean of white cloud. A spray of stars gleamed brilliantly above them. Omi turned to Indigo. She spoke in a language with a wide pitch range, rich in clicks and hisses. She was speaking Dragon, and Indigo understood her. 'I'm leaving soon, Indigo, do you want me to tell you a story before I go?'

Indigo nodded. He wasn't too old for stories.

'Smok Wawelski was a young dragon, flying over Krakow one day, when he heard the Princess Wanda singing. He fell in love with her then and there, and moved into a cave beneath the castle. He listened to the princess singing, and joined in. His songs were roars that shook the mountains. He called her name, and his fiery breath lit the night. He didn't mean to strike fear into the hearts of men. In fact he dreamed of becoming a mortal man, so the princess might love him.

'When brave knights and great warriors came to do battle, Smok realised the people of Krakow didn't want him. They were terrified of him. He knew he should go, but he couldn't bear to leave his beloved Wanda, so he fought and defeated the knights and warriors, and remained in the cave, close to his love.

'One day, a crafty tailor tricked him by leaving a sheep laced with explosives outside his cave. Smok ate it, but the resulting explosion didn't kill him. It turned him into a man. As the town rejoiced in the death of the dragon, Smok rejoiced in his new human form. He sought out the Princess Wanda, she fell in love with him, they married, and lived happily ever after.'

Omi pointed to the sky. 'Smok is coming for me.' She rose to her feet, kissed Indigo, and shuffled into the cabin, 'I need to get ready.'

'Omi …' Indigo called after her. He had so many questions.

Omi turned and smiled. 'You'll be fine, Indigo.' She nodded towards the plateau, 'Your friend is waiting for you.'

Indigo left the porch and walked across the plateau. Rue was standing in the same place they'd met the night before. 'I came to say goodbye,' she said.

'Where are you going?'

'I'm not going anywhere. You are,' she looked confused, 'aren't you?'

'No.' As soon as the word fell out of Indigo's mouth, he realised his answer was wrong. He would have to go home now. *Wouldn't he?* He thought of his home, and his family. Then he remembered the feeling he'd had on the journey, when he realised how little he'd seen of the world. 'I don't know,' he corrected.

'Aren't you going to fly off and find Ruby?' Rue laughed but it was clipped, insincere.

Indigo lifted his head and imagined flying through the black sky, surrounded by stars. He closed his eyes. The muscles in his back tensed as they lifted his wings. His wings beat against the air. The air rushed against his cheeks. He rose from the floor, weightless, and opened his eyes. 'No.' He turned to Rue. 'What are you going to do?'

Rue turned to the sanctuary. 'Stay and help Orava with the mess your grandfather left behind.'

'Mess?' Indigo questioned.

'Don't you see it?' Rue's voice heightened in anger. 'Your grandfather has thrown everything out of balance. He's always been irresponsible, creating havoc everywhere he goes. He destroyed Krakow, killing thousands of people. He brought hundreds of dangerous, uncontrollable beasts here and encouraged them to breed. Then he flies off to who knows where, abandoning your grandmother, and leaving the sanctuary spiralling into instability.'

Indigo wondered if he was shirking responsibility. 'What should I do?'

'I don't know,' Rue snapped. 'You'll probably do what all dragons do. Cause more trouble. Smok shouldn't have married your grandmother or had children.'

'You're being unfair,' Indigo retaliated.

'Am I?' Rue's eyes blazed. 'Ruby has hunted and killed thousands of animals here. Graphite has done his share of damage too, he brought the Hydra here, as a pet. And Emerald...'

'What about my mother?' Indigo cut in sharply.

'I know what she's doing in the Lakes. She's as dangerous as your grandfather.'

Indigo thought about his mother, her long walks in the mountains, their garden full of herbs, the "URGENT" and "FRAGILE" parcels she received. *Was she starting a sanctuary in the Lake District?* A tingle of excitement ran through Indigo. He thought about his cockatrice. Maybe she could start a colony there. He wondered how you trained weasels. Indigo suddenly felt protective towards his mother. 'What gives you the right to judge us?'

Rue sighed, 'I'm just trying to keep things in balance.'

'Why do you have to do that?'

'I didn't come here to talk about me. I thought you were going.' Rue scanned the horizon. She looked worried, 'I see my mistake. I got comings and goings confused.'

'I don't understand.'

'Your grandfather is coming, isn't he?'

Indigo nodded. 'Omi thinks so.'

Rue's eyes widened in alarm. 'Orava will try to kill him.' She turned and sprinted towards the sanctuary. Indigo ran after her. He couldn't keep up. She was getting further away from him, shrinking into the distance. Indigo squinted into the dim dawn light. It wasn't the distance between them, she really was getting smaller. Rue's legs shrunk into her body, her arms extended into wings, flapped, and she rose into the air. *Rue was the bat!* Her wings beat rhythmically, and she ascended the vertical face of the mountain.

Indigo reached the base of the cliff and frantically searched for the rope. Relieved when he found it, he started to climb.

Orava stood on a ledge at the entrance to the kraken cavern, a metal crossbow in one hand, his other hand protecting his face from the bat thrashing towards him. The bat dived at the crossbow and grabbed it with clawed feet. Orava smacked the bat hard with the back of his hand. The bat lost its grip, twisted in the air, and swooped away. It hovered, just above Orava, staring at him with angry yellow eyes.

Orava raised the crossbow. 'I will fire,' he threatened.

The bat lunged for the crossbow again, latched on tight, and flapped madly, attempting to wrestle it from Orava. Orava held the bow with both hands and yanked it towards him. The bat contorted its wings and body, reached for Orava's hand with its open mouth, and bit down with sharp, pointed teeth. Orava yelled, and tried to separate his bloody hand from the bat's jaws. He wriggled his hand desperately, but the bat refused to release him. Blood dripped onto Orava's shoes.

'Don't make me do this,' he shouted, his eyes moist and his finger hovering over the trigger.

The bat scrambled clumsily over the bow, struggling to remove its body from the firing line whilst keeping a grip on Orava's hand. Orava lost his balance and stumbled backwards. As he fell into the cavern the bow fired. The arrow swished out and tore through Rue's wing. Her eyes widened, and she tumbled downwards.

Indigo saw her fall, and without thinking he let go of the rope and pushed himself away from the cliff with his feet.

Searing pain ripped through his back as he plummeted. He screamed and heard a roar. Deep purple-blue wings extended either side of him, growing, stretching, catching the air, and slowing his descent.

The bat was below him, spiralling towards the plateau. Indigo reached out to her. His wings folded flush against his body, he surged downwards, caught her, and pulled her close to his chest. He curled the muscles in his back, took control of his new wings, and flew upwards, back to the kraken cavern.

Indigo landed on the lip of the cavern and looked down. Where he expected to see his shoes, great clawed feet gripped the rock. His toes were blue, scaly, and splayed, with long black claws where his toenails used to be. He put the bat down on a rocky ledge and peered into the cavern.

A glint of sunshine reflected off the crossbow when Orava raised it. Indigo opened his mouth and intense blue flames blasted out of it. Indigo reeled with shock. Orava staggered backwards, his arm raised to shield himself from the heat. Blue and purple flames rushed around him, danced in his pupils, and were swallowed by the cool, dark air of the cavern. Indigo closed his mouth. His throat burned. He breathed in slowly and watched Orava disappear into the tunnel in the cavern wall. Indigo stepped down into the cavern, his instinct was to follow him, hunt him down. His wings scraped against the rocks and he remembered Rue.

Indigo turned, folded his wings against his body, and crouched low. His claws sank into the rock like toes into moss. A shaft of sunlight broke through the clouds on the horizon and illuminated Rue's pale face. She was a girl, curled on a rocky ledge, holding her arm protectively. She smiled.

'Nice wings, Indigo.'

'Am I a dragon now?' Indigo whispered breathlessly. He rose, and lifted his wings up and out and felt the breeze flowing over them.

'No,' Rue shook her head. 'You just have a fine pair of wings,' she looked at his feet, 'some claws, and you breathe fire. Other than that, you're the same.' She tilted her head and narrowed her eyes, 'Your skin might have a bluish tinge,' she giggled.

'Why do you find this amusing?' Indigo flexed his claws out of the rock. 'I thought you hated dragons.'

'I don't hate dragons,' she retorted. 'I just think they're disruptive.' She lowered her voice, 'Sometimes I envy them.'

'Why?'

'Because they're irresponsible, carefree, and impulsive,' Rue smiled again, 'and because they can fly higher than bats.'

97

The sun rose, illuminating the peaks with golden light. The white cloud in the distance billowed and a fat wisp of it broke away and moved towards them. The sound of enormous wings beating resounded through the air. Indigo gazed at the dragon flying towards them. It was a brilliant white, with a large rectangular head, a thick, long neck, short legs dangling under a fat belly, and a long, straight tail.

The dragon descended to the cabin, slowed, and landed gracefully. Omi tottered off the porch, shaking and sobbing, her arms extended wide. Smok lay down. His scales were loose, tattered, and frayed at the edges, like fine frizzy white hair. Omi threw her arms around his neck and pressed her wrinkled cheek against his jaw. The dragon smiled, revealing huge curved teeth in a neat row – apart from the front two, which had a large gap between them.

Omi held Smok for a long time. They were both so old, so tired, shoulders curved, wrinkled, clouded, fraying. When they stood up, six knees wobbled. Omi walked with Smok towards the mountain, her hand resting on his neck.

Indigo watched them climb the steep slope and disappear into the shadows. 'Are they going to die?' The words fell out of his mouth involuntarily.

Rue looked at him like he was stupid.

'Dragons don't die. They just come and go,' she smiled, 'and cause chaos either way.'

With Special Thanks to

The Accent YA Editor Squad

With Special Thanks to

The Accent YA Blog Squad

Alix Long;

Anisah Hussein;

Anna Ingall;

Annie Starkey;

Becky Freese;

Becky Morris;

Bella Pearce;

Beth O'Brien;

Caroline Morrison;

Charlotte Jones;

Charnell Vevers;

Claire Gorman;

Daniel Wadey;

Darren Owens;

Emma Hoult;

Fi Clark;

Heather Lawson;

James Briggs

With Special Thanks to

The Accent YA Blog Squad

James Williams;

Joshua A.P;

Karen Bultiauw;

Katie Lumsden;

Katie Treharne;

Kieran Lowley;

Laura Metcalfe;

Lois Acari;

Maisie Allen;

Mariam Khan;

Philippa Lloyd;

Rachel Abbie;

Rebecca Parkinson;

Savannah Mullings-Johnson;

Sofia Matias;

Sophia;

Toni Davis

Luca, Son of the Morning

Tom Anderson

The water is warm … but can you be in too deep?

Luca loves reggae, hates his parents' rum habit, and wishes his dad could get a proper job. He also loves Gaby (though he'd never admit it to her face) so upsetting her is enough to push him into a dark place. Retreating to the local beach, as he always does when he can't sleep, watching the waves gives his life some sort of rhythm.

One night, as he lets the tide lull him, a group of figures emerge from the water and walk past him, unseeing. Spellbound by these impossible sea-men, Luca holds nightly vigils at the beach. Until one night the sailors beckon him to follow them back into the sea…

THE DEEPEST CUT
natalie flynn

'You haven't said a single word since you've been here. Is it on purpose?' I tried to answer David but I couldn't ... my brain wanted to speak but my throat wouldn't cooperate...

Adam blames himself for his best friend's death. After attempting suicide, he is put in the care of a local mental health facility. There, too traumatized to speak, he begins to write notebooks detailing the events leading up to Jake's murder, trying to understand who is really responsible and cope with how needless it was as a petty argument spiralled out of control and peer pressure took hold.

Sad but unsentimental, this is a moving story of friendship and the aftermath of its destruction.

For more information about **Sofi Croft**

and other **Accent YA** titles

please visit

www.accentya.com